SPELLBOUND

Warlocks MacGregor®

MICHELLE M. PILLOW

Michelle M. Pillow® - MichellePillow.com

Spellbound (*Warlocks MacGregor®*) © copyright 2015 - 2018 by
Michelle M. Pillow

First Electronic Printing July 2015

Published by The Raven Books LLC

Edited by Heidi Moore

ISBN-13: 978-1-62501-165-7

About Spellbound

PARANORMAL CONTEMPORARY ROMANCE

Let Sleeping Warlocks Lie…

Iain MacGregor knows how his warlock family feels about outsiders discovering the truth of their powers, its forbidden. That doesn't seem to stop him from having accidental magickal discharges whenever he's around the woman who has captured his attention. Apparently his magick and other "parts" don't seem to care what the rules are, or that the object of his affection just might be his undoing.

Warning: Contains yummy, hot, mischievous MacGregor boys who may or may not be wearing clothing and who are almost certainly up to no good on their quest to find true love.

Warlocks MacGregor® Series

SCOTTISH MAGICKAL WARLOCKS

Love Potions
Spellbound
Stirring Up Trouble
Cauldrons and Confessions
Spirits and Spells
Kisses and Curses
Magick and Mischief
A Dash of Destiny
Night Magick

More Coming Soon

Visit www.MichellePillow.com for details.

Author Updates

To stay informed about when a new book is released sign up for updates:

michellepillow.com/author-updates

To Bailey. I hope you find magick in the world.

Note from the Author

People know magic is fake—card tricks and illusions, magicians and entertainers. But there is an older magick, a powerful force hidden from modern eyes, buried in folklore and myths, remembered by the few who practice the old ways and respect the lessons of past generations.

The term "warlock" is a variation on the Old English word *waerloga*, primarily used by the Scots. It meant traitor, monster or deceiver. The MacGregor Clan does not agree with how history has labeled their kind. To them, warlock means magick, family and immortality. This book is not meant to be a portrayal of modern-day witches or those who have such beliefs. The MacGregors are a magickal class all their own.

As with all my books, this is pure fantasy. In real life, please always practice safe sex and magic.

Chapter One

PROLOGUE

"*Dè tha thu ag iarraidh?*"

"What do I want?" Jane whispered, looking around in confusion for the speaker. She was unsure as to how she'd come to be outside. One moment she'd been in bed, the next in a garden. "I'm losing my mind."

She knew this garden. She'd itched to get her hands on it ever since she'd moved to Green Vallis, Wisconsin. The plants were choking from neglect, but beneath their twisted wildness was rich soil. Most of the trees and shrubs would be salvageable—if not at their current location, then transplanted elsewhere. The grounds were expansive and had so much potential. Being located on a hill above the small town, it had ample sunlight and natural drainage when it rained. It belonged to an old mansion that had just recently been purchased after decades of sitting empty. Everyone in town knew the story of its builder— the displaced English lord. He'd been a rake or a rogue or whatever they called the rambunctiously decadent men of the time.

Despite whatever the nobleman had lacked in his personal life, he'd had a great eye for creating picturesque beauty. The property came with eighty acres of land, including part of the surrounding forest with a stream running through it and the old English landscape garden. Yes, the giant house was nice, but Jane saw it more as a backdrop to the nature surrounding it. She couldn't imagine owning eighty acres of land. The mere idea of it was a kind of what-would-you-do-if-you-won-a-million-dollars pipe dream.

"*Dè tha thu ag iarraidh!*"

Jane flinched as she found the bearer of the mysterious voice. Why was a Scottish woman screaming at her? And why was the woman's tiny frame aging so rapidly Jane could see the wrinkles forming on the pretty face as if the woman was living an entire lifetime in a single afternoon?

Jane knew she was hallucinating. What else could this be? The doctors had warned her that her mind would eventually deteriorate. Even so, this hallucination felt very familiar as if she'd lived this moment but couldn't remember it.

"*Thalla's cagainn bruis!*"

"Chew a brush?" Jane tried to translate the woman's words. It made no logical sense that she understood any of it, as she didn't speak Gaelic. She frowned, looking at an overgrown gooseberry bush a few feet from where she stood on the cobblestone path. Not knowing why she tried to obey, she lifted her arm in its direction but couldn't reach. Why couldn't she reach it?

She looked down. A light fog surrounded her legs. It held her immobile like metal shackles. Fog like shackles? She should be able to run through the fog.

"*Dè tha thu ag iarraidh?*"

"I don't know what I want," Jane answered, blinking rapidly as a wrinkled finger pointed a little too close to her nose. How could the finger be so close? The woman was nearly twelve feet away down the path near the mansion's exterior wall. Fear filled her, nearly choking the breath from her lungs. "Why can I understand what you're saying? Who are you? How did I get here? What do you want?" She remained rooted in place, like the wild overgrowth around her yearning to be saved. "I don't understand why you're yelling at me."

The aging woman's finger dissipated into mist but did not disappear. Instead, the mist surrounded Jane's head. She swatted it away, but the action only caused the mist to swirl up her nose. Around her, the plants moved, coming to animated life. They stretched and grew, aging like the now-old woman before her, then transforming into a beautiful combination of lilac and purple Scottish heather. The heady scent of flowers and honey was so strong it burned her nostrils and caused her eyes to water. Bagpipes sounded in the distance, impossibly carried on a wind that did not stir.

And then…nothingness.

Chapter Two

GREEN VALLIS, WISCONSIN, PRESENT DAY

Bagpipes. More friggin' bagpipes!

Jane Turner pressed her dirty gloves to her temples, trying to get the sound to stop. At first, it had been a call on the wind early in the mornings when she tended the plants in her nursery, so distant she assumed one of the new Scottish guys who'd moved into town was playing in their mansion on the hill that overlooked Green Vallis. Who else would suddenly be playing bagpipes if not the local Scots? She'd seen some of the MacGregors around town in kilts, and Scottish descendants always seemed to take a lot of pride in their heritage.

She could handle morning band practice. It was actually kind of relaxing and unique while she worked in her gardens. But then the music became more insistent, filling her mind at all hours of the day, becoming louder until she was humming along to a tune she couldn't possibly know. It dug into her brain like a singing earworm she couldn't get out. She'd walked the perimeter of the small piece of land that held her two greenhouses and gardens, trying to see where the men practiced. No one was there.

And then the music started at night, so loud it woke her from a dead sleep. She'd gone to her bedroom window expecting someone out on her lawn serenading her.

Ha, Jane thought sarcastically. *Someone serenading me. That will be the day pigs fly to Mars and back.*

In Wisconsin, men appeared to like three things. Football, the outdoors, and beer. No, really. It was true, and Jane had witnessed the evidence to prove it. Football season showcased bankers in state football team colors instead of classic suit choices, and locals sported foam cheese-wedge hats. Church services even let out early on game days. And, much to the local bars' bragging pride, the state had ranked the fifth highest in the nation for beer consumption, with each person drinking nearly thirty gallons in one year. Wisconsin was also ranked the highest for avidly drunk sports fanatics…or something like that.

Okay, so maybe it wasn't fair stereotyping

everyone into those categories, but Jane had yet to meet a single local who didn't enjoy such things. Jane didn't care for football or beer. She did like the outdoors, but she didn't encourage people to come into her private sanctuary. Of course, she had landscaping customers. To run a small business, she needed customers.

She had hoped the MacGregor family would hire her to tend their expansive property. Though she'd mailed flyers and the realtor who'd sold them the mansion assured her that given out her card, the family had not called her. It wasn't that she just wanted to breathe new life into the landscape—which she did—she also needed the work. Desperately.

Melancholy filled her. She'd put every penny she could scrape together into purchasing the nursery. She worked all the time, from the moment she woke up to the second she fell asleep. What else could she do? Keeping busy made her feel better.

Despite the beer and the football, she liked Green Vallis. The people were warm and friendly. Family units were strong—at least they appeared to be from her vantage point on the outside looking in. They invited her to join them, but she wasn't really good at making those kinds of friendly connections. The small town was as good of a place as someone like her could find. She didn't trust easily, and the locals accepted her quiet ways without question. For the most part, they ignored her unless they needed her services.

She dropped her hands and patted the soil. It was a needless gesture, but the firm feel of earth against her gloved palm was comforting and familiar. A light breeze stirred. Strands of her hair tickled her cheek and neck. The nature of earth and plants she understood. People were more complicated. Those complications were messy and painful.

The bagpipes became progressively louder. At first, she tried to ignore them, but the sound filled her mind and called her to her feet. Unable to help her curiosity, she started to walk. She told herself it was pointless to look. She'd already tried to find the source of the music and had been unsuccessful.

Then something new was added to the music —laughter and the muffled voices of a crowd. She pulled the gloves from her hands and tossed them on her worktable as she passed by the exterior wall of a greenhouse. Townsfolk greeted her as she walked by the building that housed her small storefront. Men dressed in formal jackets and kilts paraded over the old brick street, stepping in time to their music. Two horses flanked the bagpipers, showcasing what was obviously a family crest.

Jane held back in the shadows, simply watching their approach. A chill ran up the back of her spine, and she shivered violently. Her eyes automatically went to a group of women in tartan gowns. Fierce eyes met hers as a withered old woman stared at her from a wheelchair. The woman was being pushed by a young beauty who didn't seem to notice her charge's bony old finger lifting toward Jane.

Taking a step back, Jane tried to hide deeper in the shadows as the small parade moved down the street away from her. Camera phones flashed as people took pictures. The old woman turned, watching her with uncalled for intensity. A sense of foreboding and fear filled Jane as if she'd met the woman in a previous life. The wrinkled face and angry eyes were familiar. Jane's limbs suddenly became very heavy. What was even stranger was the fact she felt as if she deserved the woman's unhappy attention.

Age and illness were clearly taking their toll. It was only a matter of time before the woman died. Is that why the old lady stared at her? Those close to death often sensed Jane's secret. Did the woman blame her for what was naturally to come?

She wouldn't be the first dying person to look at Jane like that.

A loud bark drew Jane from her trance. She jolted to awareness as a very excited English bulldog in plaid attire trotted behind the wheelchair to lead the playing men. Jane gave a small laugh as her gaze swept toward the musicians. She'd seen a few of the MacGregor men around town and had thought them an attractive bunch, but to see them in full force was impressive. Genetics clearly ran strong in the family, as it was apparent they were each related. They all had dark hair and proud features, each as handsome as the next—from the young twenty-something hunks to the older salt-and-pepper generation.

Her laugh instantly died. Brown eyes flecked with green glanced in her general direction. She gasped and tried to press into the building. Unlike the old woman, the man's sparkling gaze caused an intense heat to erupt inside her. His hair was shorter than some of the others, and dark locks blew forward across his face. His eyes didn't meet hers. He continued to play his bagpipe, and she was glad when he moved along. Desire filled her, causing her to tremble. She didn't trust it.

"Are you keeping bees now?"

Jane turned in surprise at the question. Chef Alana had moved to Green Vallis about a year after Jane. Her business, *Perfection Restaurant*, was one of the best in town. But that didn't stop the locals from supporting her competition. Within the first year, Alana had put two of the local boys out of business. To get back at her, they'd combined efforts, opened a new restaurant and proceeded to do everything they could to sabotage Alana's business. In town, the feud was legendary.

Jane was on friendly terms with the woman. They didn't hang out or anything, but Jane would have named her as a friend if asked. "Uh…?"

"Bees. You smell like honey." Alana's question finally registered.

Jane lifted her wrist and sniffed. She did smell like honey. She tried to shake off the feelings swirling inside her. Her tone sounded a little distracted as she tried to form a coherent answer. "No, I'm allergic to bees." She dared a glance at the kilted men, but the man who'd captured her notice had marched on. "I must have brushed up against something. I was tending the vegetable garden, getting ready for the farmers market."

"Vegetables?" Alana's voice demanded her attention. "Forget the farmers market. Sell me your inventory. I'm terrified to order through the grocery store after the tainted-mushrooms incident."

"I read about that a few days ago in the

paper," Jane said. "Tainted casserole at a potluck at Sheriff Johnson's house, right?" She hadn't been invited to the potluck so had missed out. Considering most of the guests had ended up in the hospital with food poisoning, she'd deduced it was for the best she was anti-social.

"Honestly, what I remember about that night reminds me of a misspent youth." Alana gave a small laugh. "The doctors say it is temporary amnesia due to severe hallucinogens."

Jane arched a brow.

"Magic mushrooms," Alana clarified.

Jane started to give a polite laugh and then realized Alana wasn't joking. "If you're serious about needing vegetables, let me know what you want. I have more garden space I can till out back. I'll try to fulfill whatever order you need."

"I'll take you up on that." Alana studied the nearby rows of tomatoes. "How do you get them so big? Gene splicing?"

"Nothing that spectacular. I've just always had a knack for it," Jane said.

"Honestly, I want your energy secret. How do you even have time for everything?" Alana smiled. "Between the nursery, landscaping jobs and the farmers market, you can't be sleeping. Or eating. Or breathing. Let alone have any time for family."

My mother abandoned me when I was a baby. My

father is dead. My stepmother spent my inheritance. I'm all alone in the world. I'm broke because medical bills wiped out my savings. I don't really have a choice, she thought before saying aloud, "I like to keep busy, and I don't have any family to speak of."

"Well, if you need another job, I'm looking for a new waitress. Mine keep leaving for college. Actually, that's not true. The last one left me for Las Vegas."

"What's going on with this parade?" Jane changed the subject before she found herself agreeing to the extra work. She had made it her goal to pay off every single penny owed and found turning down jobs very hard to do. "I don't remember seeing anything on the town schedule."

"Callister probably knows." Alana nodded at the older woman running along the crowd with her little notebook. The way she acted, one would guess she was a paid reporter. In truth, she was a rumor-hungry busybody who stuck her nose in everyone's business.

"She's probably writing down marching violations to turn over to the band police later," Jane said. Neither of them were fans of the nuisance that was Mrs. Callister. "Someone told me she calls the police station almost daily to give her list of complaints."

"Poor Sheriff Johnson." Alana gave an

unamused laugh. "I have health inspectors in my place every month thanks to that woman, and all because I wouldn't give her a bigger senior citizen's discount. I'm not convinced she's even technically a senior. Yet I'm still supposed to give her and her entire family half off every meal."

"She prints coupons she finds on the internet from big chain stores and tries to get me to honor them," Jane said. "They're not even from this state. Half the time they're already expired when she brings them in."

"That woman is something else, a true shakedown artist." Alana motioned toward the crowd. "Come on, take a break from all your jobs. Let's follow this trail and see where it leads."

Jane glanced behind her to the quiet sanctuary of her plants but found her feet moving to make pace next to Alana. She liked the woman's company, yet that wasn't what caused her to follow. It was the music. The sound pulled her along with it.

The parade led them down a few blocks to Main Street and then turned toward the hill overlooking the town. The MacGregor mansion was on top of that hill, towering over Green Vallis like a medieval feudal lord over his villeins. She wondered what it would be like living in such a place surrounded by so many extended family members.

Most towns simply paved over their old red-brick roads, but Green Vallis had preserved theirs in the downtown area. It was one of the details that had first compelled Jane to stop her truck and walk around. The for-sale sign on the local nursery was why she'd stayed.

The bagpipers led the crowd up the hill, but instead of following the winding drive toward the mansion, they marched along the driveway of the old Victorian house owned by Lydia Barratt. The Victorian was the only other property on the hill, and Jane often envied the location of it—set up and away enough to be relatively private but close enough to the amenities of town life. Lydia had inherited the house from her grandmother and ran a small lotion business out of it called *Love Potions*. Lydia sold most of her wares online. Being as Jane owned a nursery, she had supplied Lydia with herbs on many occasions. Alana, Lydia and Jane all belonged to the same women's small business group.

"Can you imagine having these guys as next-door neighbors?" Alana whispered.

Jane's eyes strayed to the handsome bagpiper. She'd been consciously trying not to look at him. The musicians stopped in front of Lydia's home.

One MacGregor stepped away from the procession and handed his bagpipes to the elderly woman in the wheelchair.

"That's Lydia's man friend. His name is Erik MacGregor—well, obviously a MacGregor. He brought Lydia on a date to the restaurant and couldn't stop staring at her. It was very sweet." Alana directed her gaze toward Lydia's boyfriend as he met Lydia coming out of the house.

"I saw him here when I delivered those new bushes. I couldn't understand what he was saying, but I think he was reciting Gaelic poetry to her from the lawn." Jane felt a tiny chill and turned her attention to the house. She thought someone slipped past an upper story window. The movement was fleeting, and Jane forced herself to ignore it. Instead, she looked at Erik and Lydia, and then to Lydia's best friend, Charlotte, standing in the doorway watching. There was a faint flicker behind Charlotte, but the woman didn't appear to notice there was anything non-corporeal behind her. Jane changed her mind. She no longer wished to live in the old home, not if it came with ghosts.

"Lydia Barratt, *táim i ngrá leat.*" Erik took a knee. "Say ya will marry me, lassie."

Jane moved her gaze from Charlotte to the MacGregors, one of them in particular. She stared at the man's head, willing him not to look at her as the music completely faded away. There was something about him that captured her notice, causing a kind of twitch she felt in the pit of her stomach.

The sound of Gaelic words stirred in Jane's mind. She couldn't understand them, but she felt if she concentrated on the words hard enough, the meaning would come to her. The mystery man turned, hair blowing lightly to cover his eyes. She didn't want to make eye contact and took an unconscious step back to try to hide from his view. It didn't matter. The sexy Scotsman somehow found her in the crowd. The moment his gaze met hers, she pretended not to notice him.

"Aww," Alana said softly seconds before the crowd started to cheer in excitement.

Erik kissed Lydia. The woman must have said yes to him. The couple was like a romance movie —sexy hero and strong heroine finding their happily ever after. A pang of longing filled Jane at the sight. She wanted so much to have that perfect moment, surrounded by love. But she would never have that kind of connection with anyone.

"Good for them," she said to Alana. She started to touch the woman's arm only to stop when she realized her hands were dirty from work despite the fact she'd had on gloves most of the morning. "I should get back. I've been having trouble with one of my greenhouse's watering systems. I need to replace a pressure regulator."

"Come on, lads, drinks on me!" one of the older Scotsmen shouted. Cheers answered his offer. The bagpipes started up again as the group turned back down the hill.

"Oh, okay then," Alana said. "I think I'll follow this crowd to watch the antics."

Jane took a slightly different path down the hill from the others. When she glanced back, the marching lines were more chaotic, and the sound of bagpipes less in sync as the MacGregors began poking each other's instruments in mischief. A few even tried to trip each other. She walked faster, lowering her head to watch her step.

"Hey, ya know you're welcome to join us, lassie."

Jane looked up from the ground in surprise, not having expected someone to follow her. At first, she didn't answer because she wasn't sure the offer was for her. Then she didn't answer because she'd forgotten how to speak. Her mouth opened, at least she was pretty sure it did, but nothing came out. The sexy brown-eyed MacGregor smiled at her expectantly. Why was he there? She'd been very careful not to make eye contact with him.

"I know ya." The man sounded both sure and unsure at the same time. His Scottish accent was thick as if he'd just arrived in the United States. "We've met, haven't we?"

Jane tried to formulate an answer but merely ended up shaking her head in denial. She knew what he meant. He felt familiar, but she would have remembered meeting the Scottish poster boy for sex appeal.

"Oh, I must be mistaken then." He didn't sound very mistaken though. He held out his hand. "Iain MacGregor."

Jane looked at his hand a few moments longer than was socially acceptable. Slowly, she reached forward. He took her hand, but instead of shaking it, he held her fingers in his. Tingling warmth moved up her arm. She gasped as the world literally blew away to leave her alone in a strange fog.

Jane's feet became rooted to the ground. Her heart pounded as she fearfully glanced around looking for the man who'd just been there. He was gone. But even stranger was the fact she was no longer at the base of the hill heading home. She was on top of it in the MacGregor gardens. She stared at a window, feeling a pull toward it.

"Lassie?"

Jane gasped at the sound and blinked heavily. The fog was gone, and she was standing before

Iain with her hand hanging between them. He'd let her go. Small evergreens dotted the area leading down the hill, just as they should be.

"Um," she managed, confused by what had happened. "Jane. I'm Jane."

"Jane. We're all heading to the pub. Would ya like to—"

Jane didn't stay to listen. Something inside her told her to run, so she did. She headed down the hill faster than before.

Chapter Three

"Would ya like to—" Iain paused, shocked as the pretty woman turned and hurried away from him. To himself, he finished, "Get a drink with me?"

This wasn't the first time his charming self had knocked a girl speechless, but it was the first time the girl had stared at him like he was an idiot for even trying to talk to her. He had caressed her fingers, feeling that instant connection snap through his body. It was the same giddy feeling he'd had as a youth running around the Scottish countryside—the excitement beating in his heart, the nerves bunching with anticipation in his stomach, the security of home and family pumping in his veins and giving him confidence.

Only, she'd held frozen like he was trying to

give her leprosy. He lifted his hand and slowly stroked the skin where they'd touched.

Did he just get rejected?

Iain wasn't so vain as to believe every woman wanted him, but normally it took them longer than two seconds to decide. What a peculiar place the MacGregors had moved to. Iain was the third oldest child in a family of six siblings, with countless cousins, and yet in all their centuries of living, his brother Erik was the first from their generation to find true love. It had to mean something that Erik had found it here, in this town. Green Vallis called to their warlock natures. It was special.

A tiny vibration filled Iain. It came from below, like an invisible current working up from the ground through the bottom of his feet. When he closed his eyes, he heard its low hum as if the earth was trying to speak to him. This area had a wealth of natural power.

"Smooth, brother," Euann teased from behind him. "How many times do I have to tell ya, Iain? Ya are not a pretty man. I think ya aimed too high with that one. Now stop scaring our new neighbors and come get a pint. We'll find ya a nice drunk sea hag to talk to."

Iain managed not to show he was startled by his brother's approach. Turning to face Euann, he arched a brow. "Like you're anything to gander at."

Euann took the insult in stride, not losing his smile. He was the second oldest of the siblings. All the MacGregor men were able to attract women. Euann was no exception, even if he didn't look like the rest of them. People always thought he was of Latin descent, until he spoke and the accent gave his Scots away. The siblings used to tease him that their ma had made a deal with a Sack Man, a kind of Spanish bogeyman, and he wasn't really one of them. How else could they explain Euann's hatred of golf? The sport was born in their homeland after all. "So, do ya think Ma will be happy now that Erik's brought home a bride?"

Iain gave a small laugh. "If she's not, I'm offering ya up as a sacrifice as the next to fall. You're second born, so it's only fair."

"How do ya think Charlotte feels about a double wedding?" Euann looked toward the old Victorian. Iain doubted his brother was serious about Charlotte. She just happened to be pretty and best friends with Erik's new fiancée. That made her convenient. "I mean, if one can over-look the fact that your magick left the poor lassie a bit touched in the head."

"For Charlotte's sake, I hope the madness does

not last." Iain hid his frown. He didn't like being in too close of a proximity to Charlotte. It wasn't her fault, but his family had just recently finished dealing with a couple of *lidércs*. The wraithlike creatures had used Lydia and Charlotte as vessels to try and steal Erik and Iain's powers. Lydia had a rare genetic anomaly that synced her perfectly to one particular warlock. Being Erik's *inthrall* had nothing to do with love, but it did give her a natural connection to him that allowed her to borrow his magick. The fact Lydia also loved his brother made their situation very rare indeed. Lydia was Erik's *fíorghrá*, his one true love.

However, Charlotte was not Iain's anything but a new friendly acquaintance, and the *lidérc* had given the woman a potion to make her a conduit that forced Iain's powers out of him. It had hurt like hell, for his magick was his very essence, his soul. He imagined it had been the same for Charlotte, only his family had erased the woman's mind, so she didn't recall what had happened to her. It was the least they could do considering the circumstances. Erasing minds carried a lot of risks as well. Most mortals were not meant to handle the supernatural. Now she didn't even remember that real magick existed.

Iain couldn't remember how he'd survived the painful ordeal, only that he had. One moment he was on the ground, feeling Charlotte pull his life out of him. He'd been dead. Of that much he was certain. He'd felt the last moment, the last rip of his warlock soul. But then something unexpected had happened. He'd woken up, dazed and hot, staring at the open lid of an antique glass preservation coffin. Hazy memories of how that happened danced around his brain like ghosts, transparent images he couldn't grasp. Now, because of the potion the *lidérc* gave Charlotte, whenever he stood too close to her, he felt a residual pull and had to consciously restrain his magick from going to her.

"Hey," Euann said, drawing his attention back to the moment. "We won't let Charlotte turn out like Helena."

"Helena was lifetimes ago. We are better with erasing spells now." Iain didn't want to think about the past. He gave Euann a serious look. "Maybe ya should ask Charlotte to marry ya before her senses return. A woman would have to be touched in the head to take ya as a husband. Charlotte might be your only chance."

"Oh, ya have jokes now, do ya? I have no intention of getting married." Euann hooked his brother's arm and forced him toward where the elders had led the throng of locals to drink. Trust Uncle Fergus to buy a few rounds for the townsfolk. He'd been doing that little goodwill trick since the dawn of time.

"Who's joking?" Iain chuckled. "All I'm saying is, I don't think Ma can summon the amount of magick needed to make ya suave with the ladies."

"And yet I've never sent a woman running away screaming." Euann nodded his head to where the mysterious woman had disappeared.

"She wasn't screaming," Iain grumbled. Actually, Jane hadn't said much of anything. He let his eyes shift as he tried to see the beautiful woman within the tree line. The bark in the distance came into sharp focus, but he did not catch a glimpse of her.

Each warlock was born with both a gift and a curse. Iain's burden gave him one very nice bonus of exceptional eyesight. It also gave him a restless wildness he fought very hard to control. It wasn't easy knowing he had the ability to fly like the birds of prey he could transform into, yet was constantly forced to clip his magickal wings for fear he'd never find his way back to his human self.

Spells and potions could be learned, but some talents came more naturally than others. For Iain, his gift was his ability to make things grow. Warlock magick didn't just materialize from nothing. It needed fueled. They could take from nature, take the life from plants to energize their powers. Iain was able to replenish plant life, to give that energy back. It is why he was in charge of the family gardens. Life and magick were a delicate balance, and he understood it better than most. In Green Vallis, they were surrounded by nature. Here they could borrow just enough from the forest as a whole to maintain their magick without killing their surroundings.

"I don't think Ma should be working any spells right now. I'm worried about her." Euann's expression fell as he turned serious. "I know she's conjured future-telling magick before, but I've never seen it drain her this much. She looks like she just crawled out of the grave and can't even walk. Malina has to push her in that damned chair. Half the time, she doesn't remember what she was doing two seconds ago. My conversations with her loop."

"What choice did she have? Ma needed to divine the future. We needed to know if the threat against our family was over and that the *lidércs* were gone for good. We needed to know if Green Vallis was a safe place for us to relocate the entire MacGregor clan to. We need this. We've been living away from nature for too long, and it shows in our magick." Iain sighed. There were other, more practical concerns that had forced them to find a new home, like avoiding questions about their lack of aging. People started to notice when their neighbors never grew old. For the most part, the MacGregors tried to stay out of the limelight and never entered the social scene for too long.

Nature wasn't their only option. Sexual energy worked as a fuel too. It gave a surge to their magick, fierce like an orgasm, but did not sustain like natural elements—unless of course it was sex with a *fíorghrá*. True love changed everything. It's probably why finding a *fíorghrá* was so damned hard.

Iain had the strangest urge to change course and follow the mysterious Jane to see where she went. If his brother hadn't interrupted him, he might have done just that. Would it have been a mistake? She didn't seem very interested in talking to him.

"I do not need the family-responsibility speech. I know no one wants the chore of house shopping for the entire clan again, but there are other places. Ma didn't need to drain her energy divining the future," Euann said. "If Green Vallis doesn't feel safe, we move again."

Iain was also worried about their ma, but he didn't want to admit it. "Ma probably looked ahead more than was necessary. Lydia is going to be her first daughter-in-law." Lydia might be able to borrow Erik's magick, but she didn't possess any of her own. This had caused some reason for concern within the clan. Until Lydia had absorbed enough of Erik to make her one of them, she was considered fragile. "I'm sure Ma just wanted to make sure the woman was safe from future threats against her life. Between the *lidércs'* supernatural attack and her mortal stalker—"

"I know all that," Euann quipped.

"Untwist your panties, little lady," Iain said as he eyed his brother. "No reason to be all moody. The aunts will take care of our ma, and she'll regain her strength soon."

Euann nodded.

"Good. Now let's go down to the pub and meet the townsfolk," Iain said.

"Bar," Euann corrected, just to be contrary.

"Let's go down to the pub before I hit ya with a bar," Iain said, forcing himself not to follow his mystery woman.

Euann walked with him, but he didn't let the conversation drop. "We've already encountered threats here and we're not even settled."

Iain didn't answer. He didn't need to. Every MacGregor understood what was at stake. They lived for centuries because they had learned to adapt and control their environments.

"Maybe it's a sign we should move on. Erik scouted the location. Maybe his senses were off because he met his *fíorghrá*. He wants this to be the right place for us because this is where Lydia is."

"Since when do ya run from potential danger?" Iain didn't want to leave Wisconsin. He felt the power around them. This town was special. He wasn't sure how, but he knew that it was. "Such is the way with places of great power —all sorts of people, both good and bad, will be drawn here. Most won't even know why they decide to stop and put down roots."

"That's easy for ya to say. Your job is making sure we have trees." Euann glanced around the forest already full of life. "I'm the one who has to figure out the right security. I'm going to need at least fifty cameras to cover the woods."

Iain let loose a long sigh. Euann had centuries of tried-and-true warlock magick at his fingertips, and he persisted in playing with mortal technology. "Not again. Use the clan magick, brother. We don't need more footage of the elders running naked through the woods."

"I told everyone not to put the tapes in the security VCR. They were triggered to record off of motion sensors. It's not my fault the golf footage was replaced by the naked three-mile dash."

"It was the 80th US Open. I maintain ya did it on purpose."

"My point exactly. Only the eightieth. Eighty years is hardly anything. I'd understand the family holding a grudge for the last thirty-odd years if it was the 500th. Besides, it's *golf*. Man hits little ball into hole. The end."

"How are ya even related to us?" Iain shook his head with an expression of mock wonder.

"If ya want to see the game so badly, do an internet search. I'm sure it's on there."

"Ah, the internet is just a passing fad with the youngsters," Iain teased. "Soon we'll be back to gas lamps and horse power as nature intended."

"Says the man who buys the newest smartphone every six months," Euann countered.

"What can I say, I like downloading funny animal pictures," Iain defended. In truth, he kept breaking and losing them.

The walk into downtown Green Vallis briefly reminded Iain of what it felt like coming into the burghs of his youth. Though these buildings were red brick, not imposing gray-stone townhouses with slate roofs, there was a similar feel to the long main street lined with tall buildings pressed together. The fresh air and the sound of Scottish voices shouting over a noisy crowd awakened a deep memory of simpler times. He paused, closing his eyes as he listened to Euann's steps moving away from him.

An ache filled him, one he didn't let himself feel too often. Sometimes, he wished time would stand still and be quiet. When you had a life expectancy of hundreds upon hundreds of years, human life became fleeting in comparison. It wasn't just losing mortal friends. It was the customs, technology, fashion, architecture, everything. Existence was ever changing and fluid. Maybe that was why he liked plants. Their evolution seemed slow compared to society.

A breeze stirred around him, lifting his kilt and dropping it against his legs. He focused his hearing on Euann first, then the crowd, the creak of a door, the jingle of a bell. Next, he searched for a sign of the woman, but he could not determine her whereabouts.

Smiling slowly, he opened his eyes. Something about Jane reminded him of his youth. It had been a long time since he'd been captured by a mystery. He had time to unravel this one. Green Vallis was a small town. Jane couldn't hide from him for too long.

Chapter Four

"Idiot." Jane scolded herself. "You had one of the MacGregors right there, willing to talk to you, and you could have at least tried to act normal and land yourself a decent paying job. So what if he's handsome. You shouldn't hold that against him. You're not trying to date him. You only want to get your hands on his gardens. You're trying to get paid."

A tiny voice in her head that she couldn't seem to control answered, *You want to get your hands on his garden? Is that what Scotsmen are carrying under their kilts these days?*

She paused, glancing behind her while contemplating if she could turn around and accept the offer for a drink. "Oh, shut up, brain. Now I'm the crazy lady talking to herself again."

There was no graceful way to resume a conversation with Iain, so she continued down the hill. Besides, Iain was definitely not the MacGregor she wanted to do business with. The sound of his voice had turned her insides to mush and made her hallucinate being in a Scottish field.

The hallucination worried her, but it didn't frighten her as it would have most people. She was living on borrowed time as it was. The doctors had warned her there would be symptoms as her body deteriorated. They'd given her a year to live, even though they couldn't pinpoint what was wrong with her. She'd well surpassed that prognosis.

"Dammit, Jane," she swore as she thought of the man's alluring smile. The last thing Jane needed in her life was complications. "Stupid. Stupid. Stu—"

Jane stiffened as goose bumps washed over her. Trying not to react, she forced her feet to keep moving. She hoped the ghosts from Lydia's house hadn't followed her. Why did she have to look directly at them?

"Stupid."

Just because she could glimpse through the veil, didn't mean she wanted to. If she ignored the spirits, they would go away, as long as they didn't suspect she could see them. Jane walked faster, hoping it was a residual haunting who wouldn't know she passed. Residual spirits just replayed the same scene from their life, repeatedly, unaware of what they'd become and of the people who passed by them.

Jane wasn't so lucky. The chill followed her as she strayed off her direct path. She'd stumbled upon what was called an intelligent haunting, a ghost that was aware. Sometimes, spirits followed people around when they were bored. Though ghosts were normally locked to a location and couldn't move about too freely, there were some who figured out how to break out of their boundaries. Jane imagined that, for them, watching the living was much like having their own personal reality television show. It was time for her current undead stalker to change the channel. If she was boring enough, the ghost would lose interest and flutter away.

Bagpipes. Ghosts. Hallucinations. Walking fantasy in a kilt. Jane didn't need this. All she wanted to do was keep her head down, work hard enough to run her nursery, and that's it. The end. She didn't have any grand aspirations beyond that. Work was honest. Loneliness was safe. And when the time came, she wouldn't leave anyone to grieve her.

She turned again, correcting her course

toward the nursery. The chill stayed with her, keeping pace. She lowered her eyes and walked faster. Why wouldn't it leave?

"We know a secret," a voice whispered in her ear, startlingly loud.

Jane jolted in surprise. The ghost giggled, having caught her reaction. She turned to face the apparition, but it faded before she could get a good look at it. A streak of darkness ran away from her and disappeared completely.

"Stupid," Jane berated herself. "Stupid. Stupid. Stupid."

"LITTLE JANE, there you are, dear. Did you think you could outrun your fate forever?"

Seeing Jane try to avoid a couple of child ghosts was quite amusing to the *bean nighe* as she watched from her perch in a tree. A feeling of relief and excitement came over the old being. In all her imagining, she never would have guessed Jane had ended up in Wisconsin. But this place would do as well as any other. She wondered how Jane had managed to heal herself so well, but it didn't matter. Soon, the *bean nighe* would feed.

"Come here, children," the *bean nighe* whispered. Instantly, the two ghosts blurred and came toward her as commanded. They materialized from their dark shadows to stand as the perfect vision of innocence. White matching dresses with blue stripe trim encased pale, translucent skin. Their petticoat skirts fell to their knees to reveal ankle-high boots. Sweet smiles and cherub cheeks belied the mischief in their little brown eyes. Dark blonde ringlets framed their faces in large curls. "What are you doing out here all alone?"

One of the girls' smiles widened, and she glanced at her twin. They didn't speak.

The *bean nighe* hoped down from her perch. The girls dissipated before the creature landed on them and reappeared, holding hands, a few feet away.

"Why do you follow her?" the *bean nighe* asked.

In a singsong voice, one girl answered, "She is on borrowed time. Soon, she will be sleeping fine."

Laughing the old creature nodded. "Come, children. Show me where you live. I can see it takes a lot of energy for you to be out here, and I think we have much to discuss."

The other girl warned in the same eerie tune, "We're not bound anymore. We're not leaving like before."

"Oh, my little darlings," the *bean nighe* said, "I wouldn't dream of sending you away."

They giggled in response and began to run across the clearing, fading into nothingness.

Chapter Five

"Brilliant!" Malina laughed and clapped her hands. Even though she carried an English accent, she was a MacGregor. Like all the MacGregors, she had dark hair and eyes, but since Euann had tampered with her shampoo, her hair currently had streaks of silvery white in it. Until the prank spell wore off, she'd be coloring her hair dark every morning to hide the reemerging gray.

Iain ignored his sister as he focused on the bar napkin he'd magickally formed into a little swordsman. His paper champion wielded a green plastic cocktail pick sword at his cousin Rory's little soldier.

"Get him," Malina ordered quietly though neither combatant knew who she cheered for.

The MacGregor men were overprotective of

Malina. She hated it. Rory and Iain had boxed her in at a table along the wall of the bar as an unnecessary precaution. If any male wanted to talk to Malina, they'd have a whole clan to get through first.

Iain's swordsman slashed the weapon over his opponent's napkin stomach.

"Hey, no fair, bird boy," Rory protested. "Ya should stick to feathers and flying because ya can't swing your weapon like that. It's clear that is no Viking broadsword. Have a little respect for the art of swordplay."

"Ya are just mad my guy is winning," Iain whispered in return.

"I am—" Rory's protest was cut off as Malina slammed her palm down on the napkin warriors.

"Incoming." She swiped her hand to the side and wadded the evidence of their play as an elderly gentleman came up behind them to thank them for the free drinks. The bar wasn't anything special. It smelled of old beer and dust and had wood paneling on the walls. There were the requisite pool table and dartboard, bad neon-lit signs and beer flyers on each table. Yet, for what it was —a bar in a small town—it served its purpose.

When the man left, Euann joined them and slapped Iain on the shoulder. To Malina, he said,

"Hey, old lady, did Iain tell ya about his new girlie-friend?"

Malina arched a brow and unconsciously touched her gray-streaked hair. "Oh, paybacks are coming, brother, trust in that."

Euann laughed, unconcerned. Over the centuries, boredom often led to familial pranks. This wasn't the first, and it wouldn't be the last. In fact, Malina might bide her time for the next one, waiting a hundred years for the perfect revenge.

"I don't have a girlie-friend," Iain grumbled. He made his crushed swordsman crawl wounded toward Malina for help before doing a couple of death quivers.

Malina plucked the umbrella pick out of her drink and bit off the pineapple chunk before conjuring a paper lady in a Victorian gown. She handed the lady the umbrella and made her walk, hips swaying, toward Iain. He swiped his hand in the air to knock the napkin lady over. Malina made a small noise of affront before magickally standing the woman back up and having her stab Iain in the back of his hand with the sharp end of the umbrella.

"Ow." Iain snatched his hand away before crushing the moving sculpture beneath his flat hand and wadding it in his fist.

"So barbaric." Malina chuckled. "And that's why you will never have a girlfriend."

"Better a Scottish barbarian than an English rose," Iain teased.

The North Berwick witch trials had made it a necessity to get Malina out of Scotland when she was born. She'd been raised in England and, though hundreds of years had passed since her birth, she still carried the British ways—unless she was mad. Malina had a fierce temper, and when it flared her Scottish accent came flying out. "Better a rose than a pain in my ars—"

"So what's this about a girlie-friend?" Rory interrupted.

"Iain tried to talk to a chick." Euann laughed. "It did not go well. She ran away from him practically screaming in fear."

Rory gave Iain a mournful look. "Well, Iain, what did ya expect? Ya are not a pretty man."

"I tried to tell him," Euann said.

"Enough. A man does not have to take this abuse. I'm going for a walk." Iain finished his dirty vodka martini and set the glass down. With the mention of his mystery woman, he found he wanted to find her. There was something about her that called to him.

"Aw, we're just teasing," Euann called as Iain

walked out the door. Laughter followed the statement. Iain wasn't insulted by his family's joking.

With all the private residences, businesses, parks and streets in Green Vallis, Iain wasn't sure how he'd find her. Logically, he wouldn't. It was a good thing he didn't have to rely solely on logic. Taking a deep breath, he let instinct guide him. Magick would lead him where he wanted to go. He cleared his mind and just let his feet wander.

Chapter Six

"Hello?"

Jane whipped her head up and stiffened at the male voice. On instinct, she looked for a place to hide. Since she was outside, she couldn't really crawl underneath a tomato plant.

"Janey?"

Slowly, she looked behind her. "Sean. How did you…? What are you…?"

The last time she'd seen her stepbrother was at her father's funeral. They'd never been very close. He was older than her though to look at his perfectly chiseled face one would never guess. He had the kind of features that looked early twenties, not forties. As a teenager, he'd been athletic and beautiful. Jane had been sickly and underweight. There was an easy charm to Sean's smile and manners that made him instantly likable. At first, Jane had been very fond of him. He'd been nice to her. That was before she'd learned the hard lessons of human nature. His niceness was a façade, and she'd mistaken it as caring.

Now, seeing his white-blond hair and piercing blue eyes left her cold. The same easy smile was there, spread over his face like a mark in time, bringing her back to childhood. Her stomach began to ache, tightening in knots. She remembered what it was like to be too weak to stand up, to be too tired to turn over in bed.

"Sis!" Sean spread his arms and came toward her. She didn't move as he hugged her. Confusion set in. Why was he hugging her? What was he doing here?

"Sean, how did you find me?" Jane leaned away, and he let her go.

His smile faltered some, but he didn't let it drop completely.

"What are you doing here?" She looked over his shoulder. "Is Dana with you?"

"I'm so sorry, Jane, but I come with bad news. Mother is dead. I tried to find you before she passed, but you're a hard woman to track down." Sean paused as if waiting for her words of sympathy.

"Dana is dead?" Jane tried not to let her relief

show. At least her stepmother wasn't out front waiting in the car.

"She talked about you a lot at the end. She missed you. We tried very hard to find you." Sean made his way over to her garden and seemed to study the evenness of the rows. "She was so good to you, you know?"

"Uh, yes," Jane whispered. If by *good* he meant her stepmother always smiled and gave her gifts, then yes, Dana had been good to her. Too bad smiles and new shoes didn't equal love.

Dana's life had been more of a performance for others. She'd been obsessed with presenting the perfect family. When Jane had been at her worst, Dana had insisted on carting her wheelchair around the neighborhood so others could see just how loving of a stepparent she was. Jane had been forced to endure every bone-jarring, painful bump in the sidewalk.

"Not everyone is born pretty, so those who aren't must work harder at being agreeable," Dana had instructed her on one such outing. Jane had just gotten out of the hospital, was twenty pounds underweight and had spent the night vomiting.

Oh, but who cared about all that sick stuff. Surely my unfortunate ugly ass could have been more agreeable for my neighborhood performance, Jane thought sarcastically.

The memories rushed at her, and she tried to

push them down. It was the past. She didn't want to let it into her present.

"She was certainly the only mother you had since your own mother ran off on you when you were born. Do you ever hear from her? Your mother?"

He wanted to talk about her mother? Jane didn't answer.

"Any idea where to find her?"

Jane slowly shook her head in denial. "No clue."

"So you never hear from her? Not even an address?"

"No."

"No idea at all?"

"Why are you asking me about this?" Jane prayed she was hallucinating again and that he would simply vanish and take his awkward conversation with him.

"Making conversation," Sean said. "Your mother was a runner too. My mother never blamed you for inheriting that trait. You can't help you come from a family of runners."

Jane closed her eyes and willed him to disappear. No such luck.

"She didn't blame you for never contacting us. After your father died, you were grieving." Sean placed a hand on her shoulder and nodded in understanding. "Mother was thoughtful like that."

Jane knew there were polite things she should say, things she should probably ask, but the shock of seeing him after so long had caused social etiquette to leave her.

"I'm sorry you lost her," Jane managed, the condolence coming a little later than it should have.

"*We* lost her." Sean's eyes narrowed and hardened. It was a subtle change most people wouldn't notice, but she knew this man. "We are still family."

"Sean, I..." What could she say?

"It's okay, Janey. You must be in shock. But we have each other. It's what she would have wanted," he assured her. Turning around to look at the nursery, he nodded. "You live here alone?"

"Yes."

"It's quaint."

"It suits me," she said, not sure if he'd meant it as a compliment or not.

"I'll be in town for at least a couple of weeks."

Jane knew he wanted her to invite him to stay with her, but she couldn't bring herself to extend the offer. The two-minute family reunion they'd just had would last her another five years, if not longer. She just wanted him gone. "Are you staying at the Dorchester House or one of the motels by the highway?"

"Dorchester. It will be nice catching up with my little sister. We'll have plenty of time to spend together." Sean touched her cheek. "It will be just like old times."

Jane really hoped not. Before she could answer, she realized they were being watched. Iain MacGregor stood next to the building, still wearing the kilt from the earlier parade. He wasn't exactly who she wanted to see at the moment, but considering it was either Iain or Sean, the choice was clear.

"Sean, I have to help a customer. Maybe we can catch up later over dinner?"

Sean glanced at Iain and frowned. "Sure, Janey. I'd like that very much." He moved to leave but paused to give Iain a once over. The men's eyes locked, and their expressions hardened as they stared at each other. It might have only been for a few seconds, but it was enough.

WHEN IAIN HAD FINALLY STOPPED WANDERING, he stood before the small nursery they had marched past during their parade. He remembered being compelled to return. Apparently, his magick thought now was a good time.

The front of the building resembled a two-story cottage. By the curtains on the second story, he imagined the owner lived upstairs. He'd watched the windows for movement but didn't detect any. It was the sound of voices that urged him to go around back.

Irritation burned inside of him as he watched the man touch his mystery woman's cheek. The gesture was intimate, but Jane's expression didn't seem to encourage the attention.

Ex-boyfriend? Unwanted admirer? Luckily, Sean excused himself before Iain had to summon a tree limb to reach out and drag the guy away. The little staring contest the man had tried to initiate had been laughable. With one flick of his hand, Iain could have directed enough energy at Sean to send him flying. His hand flexed now as he watched the man walk away. It was tempting. The sound of Jane's voice stopped him.

"Mr. MacGregor, how can I help you?"

Iain smiled, instantly forgetting all about Sean. Traces of dirt marred her skin and strands of her curly hair framed her face. There was an earthy appeal to her jeans and work shirt. Jane looked nothing like the women he normally dated. Considering Iain quickly lost interest in the women he dated, he'd say that was one thing in Jane's favor.

He didn't answer right away. She remained standing by her garden, eyeing him from the depths of her brown gaze with a kind of wariness that caused any attempts he would make at pleasantness to falter. Silence surrounded them. No wind, no birds, no cars on the street, nothing but the stillness punctuated by the sound of his own breath leaving his lungs.

He couldn't move. No part of him wanted the moment to end. After a couple of minutes, he realized they still hadn't spoken. Iain ran his hands through his hair, dropped his head forward and grinned at the ground. He felt like a young lad talking to his first pretty noblewoman—the fluttering in his chest, the tightening in his stomach, the pure adrenaline that fueled his magick and made him want to shoot fireballs from his fingertips. "Sorry. I must have had too much to drink."

She didn't answer.

"I suppose I should tell ya, lassie, that I'm here to buy something, but that would be a lie. I was drawn to see ya." The bumbling honesty surprised him. Not only did he feel like some greenhorn, he was acting like one too. "That was my brother who proposed to the local girl. Is she a friend of yours? Perhaps, if ya like, we could arrange a double date."

Still nothing.

Iain finally lifted his eyes to face her. She hadn't moved. Not even to breathe.

"Petrified?" Iain glanced around to see who might have cast a petrifying spell. It would be just like one of his brothers to tease him by messing with the poor woman. Leaves didn't move, not even to quiver on the branch. Insects held frozen in the garden. It wasn't just Jane that had become a statue, it was everything. Time had stopped.

The earth beneath him hummed. Energy and magick flowed through his veins. *He'd* made time stop. As he'd gazed at her beautiful face, the fleeting thought that he'd like to look at her for hours had passed through his mind. Apparently, his magick had taken its cue and made it happen. But how? That kind of spell took a lot of fuel to make it work, much more than the rows of tomatoes he'd caused to droop.

Iain took a deep breath and released his hold. Instantly, a breeze hit him, and Jane coughed lightly.

"Not again," she whispered. Jane blinked several times and looked around before sighing in relief. When she faced him, she stiffened as if just remembering he was standing there. "I apologize, Mr. MacGregor—"

"Iain," he corrected.

"I haven't been sleeping and I must have spaced out. My stepbrother just delivered some family news and…" She dusted her hands on her jeans. The gesture looked automatic. "Have you come about the landscaping services? I'll admit I would love to get my hands on your box elders. They've been left unattended for so long they're starting to take over the perimeter of the gardens. Tree roots can wreak havoc on old stones."

"Ah, aye, I need help. The family left me in charge of the grounds, and I don't know the first thing about…" Iain stopped himself from outright lying. Just great. He'd intended to ask her out on a date, and instead he was trying to hire her so he could play boss. No offense to non-magicks, but their way of caretaking tended to take a lot longer than a few spells and energy exchanges.

Iain smiled as an idea struck him. Actually, the non-magick way would be perfect. She'd be at his house all the time. Maybe then he could charm a smile out of her with the thought of something other than box elder trees.

"Do you have an idea of what you would like to have done?" Her face lit up, and she seemed to relax as she came closer to him. "I would recommend preservation over demolition. If we keep and tame down the plants that are already established, it will be much cheaper. Some can be moved and replanted. The cobblestone paths can be repaired. They obviously won't look like new, but they are original to the design, and I think there is charm to the old—"

"I was thinking a swimming pool and giant slab of concrete," he teased, interrupting her rapidly processing ideas. "Just mow it all down."

Her mouth opened, and she looked horrified. "I, ah, I…"

"I'm joking, lassie."

"Oh." She gave a nervous laugh. "Of course."

She apparently didn't think he was very funny.

"Though we will be putting in a driving range, and there are a few other family requirements. I'm warning ya, we can be a demanding lot."

"It's your home. You have every right to make it the way you want it."

"The key is to come to me if the others start making annoying demands. I'll handle them for ya." Iain gave her a charming smile and waited for a reaction.

Blush? Smile? Anything?

Jane merely nodded. "All right."

"When can ya start?" Iain found himself mesmerized by the gentle slope of her neck where it met her shoulder. Her shirt collar pulled just enough to the side to give him a peek. He'd bet the warmth of her skin would cause his lips to tingle if he kissed her there. The closer she came to stand by him, the more aware he was of his attraction to her. He felt her pulling him in like a magnet, drawing the magick from the tips of his nerve endings. Unlike Charlotte, who had painfully ripped his powers from him, Jane sweetly beckoned them.

As the invisible threads forced him closer, he could barely breathe. Their bodies had not touched, but it didn't matter. Magick revealed the press of her form to his, the stirring of her breath in an imagined kiss, the awkward hesitation of new lovers. His arousal thickened beneath his kilt. There was something familiar to his impressions of her, of her mouth, her eyes, as if they'd done this dance before, in another life, another time. After over hundreds of years, he was bound to forget many things, many people, but surely he would remember her, *this*?

"Perhaps it would be easier if you give me an idea of where you'd like to begin." Her breathing deepened. She had to feel the attraction sparking between them. How could she not? "That way I can draw up proposals and we can go from there."

"Ya smell like honey," he said.

"I'm allergic to bees," she whispered.

"I'll do my best not to sting ya, love." Iain leaned in for the kiss. Doing so felt natural and right. She didn't pull away as he lifted his hand to touch her cheek. The tips of his fingers brushed her warm skin the same moment his lips met hers.

Jane gasped loudly and tossed her head back. Confused, he jerked his mouth away in time to see her eyes rolling back in her head. On instinct, he caught her and lifted her into his arms. Her body jerked violently a couple of times before going limp.

"Jane? Jane, wake up. Please, wake up." Iain gave her a little shake. She didn't rouse. *"Ma 'se ur toil e,* Jane."

Chapter Seven

Jane bit her lip and tried not to cry. Why was this happening to her? The delusions were becoming too real. First, she hallucinated the handsome Iain leaning to kiss her, and now she was on her back in a forest unable to sit up. A nearby stream trickled, punctuated by a rhythmic scrubbing on metal —*wroosh, wroosh, wroosh*—in a steady tempo.

This delusion was new.

Wroosh. Wroosh.

Jane weakly turned her head to the side and found an old woman in a tattered dress by the stream. Thin arms worked feverishly, scrubbing clothes against an old washboard. Another ghost locked in a moment?

"You can't hide, you can't seek, you can't find the will to speak." The children's singsong voices chanted from behind the trees. Jane tried to sit up but couldn't. Giggling sounded. The scrubbing became louder. The children's song continued, "You don't belong anymore. You should not be in that form."

If she just waited it out, the voices would stop. The delusions always stopped. The creepy giggling became louder, the sound carrying from several directions at once, echoing off the trees. Jane glanced at the washerwoman. The old lady continued to work as if her entire existence hinged on scrubbing that one cloth. Gray hair flew about her shoulders in the breeze, freed from the falling bun at the nape of her neck.

"You are on borrowed time. Soon you will be sleeping fine." The children sounded closer.

Wroosh. Wroosh. Wroosh. The scrubbing quickened and became louder. Something kept drawing Jane's eyes to the old woman by the stream.

"We know your secret," a young girl whispered in her ear. Jane couldn't see the spirit, but she felt the cold chill of its breath on her cheek. It hit her like ice.

Jane gasped, finally able to sit up. Breathing hard, she looked around a lush bedroom. Would the hallucinations never end? The white walls, woodwork, and bookshelves were pristine. High ceilings towered over her, an intricate arching of dark wood showcasing a large chandelier. Nothing made sense. The books on the shelf were well kept, and the antique leather bindings indicated they were expensive. Blue and silver accents appeared in the coverlet, the closed curtains, the wide reading chair, and ottoman.

Tears filled her eyes. She had known this was a possibility. The doctors had said her mind might deteriorate. All they could do was manage the symptoms as they happened. But since they didn't know what was wrong with her, there wasn't anything else they could do but send her for more tests. The closest she'd come to an answer was that she had some kind of rare genetic disease that didn't yet have a name. Rare disorders didn't receive funding for research because not enough people had them.

She'd known the end would come sooner rather than later. The fact she'd managed a reprieve from her illness for so long was a miracle. Paying off those medical bills had become her purpose in life, a goal before she died to leave the world unburdened by her passing. The nursery gave a means to accomplish that purpose, which made her feel better. It was probably a stupid goal, but what else could she live for? It wasn't like Jane could have a husband and kids, knowing she would abandon them like her mother had abandoned her child and husband. Jane used to wonder if her mother left because she knew her daughter was sickly. Not that it mattered now.

Jane had come to terms with her shortened years. She couldn't risk someone like Dana swooping in to take care of those she left behind. Besides, if what she had was genetic, let that gene die with her.

What Jane didn't expect was to feel so lucid in her delusion. Her mind was clearly playing tricks on her—singing ghosts, a washerwoman, Iain MacGregor about to kiss her. Yeah, that kiss was clearly a hallucination, a nice one, but a hallucination nonetheless.

An orange glow caught her attention. Where did the fireplace come from?

"You're awake."

Jane directed her attention to the doorway. Iain. And he still wore his parade attire.

"I've had ladies fall into my arms before when I tried to kiss them, but none have fainted." Iain gave a small laugh as he glanced to the floor.

"I fainted?" She blinked slowly, confused. Was this real or a delusion? For lack of a better test, she pinched her forearm. She felt it. Iain smiled. She pinched herself a second time just to be sure. "What am I doing here?"

"I carried ya. I couldn't very well just leave ya

on the ground." He stepped inside and swung the door closed behind him. His presence suddenly made the spacious room feel very small.

"I live at the nursery." She sat up straighter on the bed.

"I didn't have a key." Did his voice dip? "And a fainting spell didn't seem to warrant a trip to the hospital. Your vitals were good. I brought ya here so I could keep an eye on ya."

"My vitals? Are you in healthcare?" When she rubbed her hand nervously over her leg, she realized she still wore her dirty work clothes. "Oh, your bed, I'm sorry, I..." She scrambled off the side.

"It's only a little dirt. I'm the one who laid ya down on my bed." Surely he didn't mean that to sound as intimate as it did? "And, no, I'm not in healthcare though my family does own a medical supply business and my Aunt Cait has a gift for healing."

Jane's heartbeat quickened. She was alone with Iain in his bedroom. The intimacy of that fact was not lost on her. It had been a very long time since she'd allowed herself to be alone with a man. It was a pity too since she'd enjoyed sex. When faced with mortality, it was only natural to appreciate anything that made her heart race and mind soar.

"Why did you try to kiss me?" she asked. Her breathing deepened. Attraction wound through her, awakening her body. An invisible force pulled her toward him. She obeyed the silent command and walked to stand before him. His nearness felt familiar as if she'd stood like this before.

"I don't know. It felt like the thing to do." He lifted his hand and hesitated. "Ya aren't feeling lightheaded, are ya? Not going to faint?"

Jane gave a small laugh. "I think I'm good."

Iain smiled as he leaned over to test his mouth against hers. The second their lips touched, she felt a breeze rushing against her. When he pulled back, it stopped. She shivered, entranced by his eyes. His hand still hovered near her face.

"What are we doing?" she whispered, well aware of how insane this was. Jane didn't know this man. It might feel like she did, but logic told her he was a stranger.

What does it matter? she thought. *It's not like I have time to waste by taking things slow.*

"If ya have to ask, I didn't do it right." Iain kissed her a second time, pressing harder. His lips parted, and the warm probe of his tongue poked beyond the boundary of her mouth. As he moved against her, slow and deliberate, she swore she heard the sound of bagpipes and felt the wind. Jane closed her eyes, fighting to stay in the moment, to not fall into another hallucination.

The brush of his fingers glided down her cheek and neck. Tingling erupted where he touched, teasing her with the raw desire it left in its wake. She'd ached for human contact. It had been so very long since she'd been held. Seeing her stepbrother had made the past rush forward, reminding her of what it had been like to be bedbound. This might be her last chance to be with a man before the illness came back.

I can't waste time.

I don't have the time to waste.

IAIN WASN'T sure what possessed him take Jane home with him, or why he chose to sneak her up to his bedroom. A hospital would have made sense...if he was human. Perhaps it was selfishness. His magick recognized her, whispering that he needed to protect her. As he'd held her, her body flopping in his arms, he hadn't wanted to let her go. Besides, doctors would wonder why he was carrying around an unconscious townswoman.

Or was it he was just attracted to her and making up excuses?

As she gave a soft moan and caressed up

his arms, he was pretty sure he had his answer. This woman made him horny as hell. His cock lifted with a rock-hard response. He couldn't remember a time when he had felt so frenzied, so desperate to end the ache in his body. He tugged at her clothes. His fingertips tingled, his powers begging him to magickally melt the barrier to explore the soft flesh underneath.

Jane pulled him closer as she led him to the bed. Her mouth stayed on his. She lifted his kilt, touching the backs of his thighs and under curve of his ass.

"Nae!"

The sound of his ma's voice hit his libido like a bucket of ice water. He automatically let go of Jane and pulled away from her. Turning to the door, he was surprised to see his ma out of her wheelchair. She appeared frail and swayed on her feet, but there was nothing weak about her expression. She glared at Jane.

"Get away from my son, death's *reipseach*. I know what ya are," Margareta MacGregor shouted in warning as she pointed a wobbly finger at Jane. "*Thalla's cagainn bruis. Thalla's cagainn bruis!* I will protect my house from your master. Ya cannot have my son!"

"Ma," Iain said, part in surprise, part in

warning and part in worry. "What are ya doing? Get out of here."

His ma began yelling at him in a long string of Gaelic, chiding him for bringing the woman home, cursing the woman and threatening to cast a spell on her.

"Ya are in no condition to do such a thing," he told her. His ma could barely manage to wield her fingers to pick up a cup, let alone summon the power it would take to throw Jane to the trolls.

"I'll go," Jane said, pushing past him. She paused, unable to leave while his ma blocked the door.

"Jane, I'm sorry, she's not well. She—" Iain tried to explain his ma's strange behavior.

"No, it's all right. I have a lot of work waiting for me back at the—" Jane flinched as Margareta swung a hand at her.

Iain, unsure what else to do, swooped his ma in his arms and held her struggling form as Jane bolted for the door. The sound of her running footsteps faltered, and he heard Rory exclaim, "Easy, beautiful, not that I mind holding ya, but I usually get a name first."

Iain grumbled in frustration and set his ma down. "I'll deal with ya in a moment."

By the time he made it to the hall, Rory was following a running Jane down the stairs.

"Seriously, lassie, tell me which one of my kin scared ya and I'll be sure to hex them good," Rory offered.

Iain muscled Rory out of his way as he tried to catch Jane, who was heading out the front door.

"Hey, I saw her first!" Rory protested. Just as Iain's feet landed on the reception hall floor, Rory hit him in the back with a small electrical charge. It was only a small burst of magick, more playful than painful, but it was enough to cause him to trip forward and fall against the wall.

"Death's *reipseach!*" Margareta screeched, toddling toward the stairs as if she would give chase.

Iain wanted to go after Jane, but while she was technically unharmed, his ma looked like she was about to fall over.

"Uh, Iain, why is Aunt Margareta calling that woman a hussy?" Rory crossed his arms over his chest and chuckled. "What did we tell ya about bringing prostitutes home?"

Iain growled. He gestured at his ma as he made his way to catch her. "Shut up, Rory. Stop my ma, she's about to fall."

Rory turned and swept his arm forward to stop the frail woman from tumbling down the staircase. "Easy there, Aunt Margareta. Where do ya think you're going?"

"*Reipseach*," the woman insisted.

"I know, I know, *reipseach.* Iain did always have questionable taste in women." Rory turned to wink at Iain as he led Margareta down the hall to find her wheelchair. His ma was clearly out of her mind. The aftereffects of her future casting were worse than any of them had thought. "The bad lassie is gone now. Your work is done. Time to rest."

Iain stopped halfway up the stairs, letting Rory handle his ma for fear she'd become worked up again if he tried to help her. Sitting down on a step, he gave a weak laugh. To himself, he said, "Well, I sure know how to show a girl a good time."

Twice he'd watched Jane run away from him. Once she fainted. For a glorious moment, she'd kissed him. And that was all in one day.

A small smile formed on his mouth. He was suddenly very eager to see what tomorrow would bring.

Chapter Eight

Jane liked the serenity of night. Okay, truthfully, she liked hiding like a coward all evening in case Sean came back to take her to dinner. If he couldn't find her, he couldn't guilt her into spending time with him. If she didn't spend time with him, she wouldn't have to listen to how great Dana was and how ungrateful of a stepdaughter she'd been. Or the weird questions about her birth mother. Jane had no idea what had prompted him to ask about it. She could only conclude with his own mother passing, he had moms on the brain.

"Cowardice for the win," Jane mumbled to herself. "I'll hide until he goes away."

As the hours ticked on, she knew she should be sleeping, but if she tried to lie down, she wouldn't be able to stop thinking of Iain. Though

the end of their time together had been morti-
fying—a kind of high school nightmare where
you're caught making out by the boy's parents—
the kiss leading up to it had been delightful.

Growing up, boys had not been into dating the
sick girl. So when she'd been well enough to date,
she'd dated. A lot. Being faced with her own
mortality had a way of bringing things into sharp
perspective. There wasn't much time to do
anything, so at one point she had tried to do
everything.

The melody of the night forest played around
her, so peaceful and quiet. She had given up
whining about how life wasn't fair. Fear still
lingered in the back of her mind, fear of death,
fear of the unknown, fear she would become a
ghost, but she had years to make her peace with
that. If she did haunt this place, she hoped it was
her greenhouses and surrounding lands. That
wouldn't be a bad eternity. Then maybe, centuries
from now, she would simply fade away, her energy
dissipating into the landscape.

"Iain MacGregor," she whispered, looking up.
The woods were quiet. Strips of moonlight shone
through tree limbs that reached like surreal black
fingertips across her vision. A single tear slid down
her cheek. She touched her mouth, imagining his
kiss.

Taking a small pocketknife out of her cargo pants, she looked about. A mystic had once told her that if she left pieces of herself around while she lived, it would expand her haunting territory when she died. Jane wasn't sure she believed in sideshow magic tricks—or the *Old Magick* as the mystic had spelled it on her sign. She had no idea what had possessed her to talk to the palm reader and ask about ghosts. Still, just in case, she was leaving her stamp all over the woods.

She cut her palm and pressed it to a nearby tree under a branch. Holding the wound to the rough bark stung at first, but then it made her feel better. This forest wouldn't be a bad eternity.

The sound of running feet erupted behind her, and she stiffened. No one ever came out here at night. She'd walked the woods hundreds of times. Her mind instantly went to the creepy girl ghosts chanting by the stream.

"Whoo hoo!"

Jane whipped around, startled as a streak of naked flesh sprinted past her. The Scottish voice was met with loud cheers from those who followed him. "Water's this way, lads, or my name isn't Raibeart MacGregor, King of the Highlands!"

Another naked man dashed through the forest after him. "It smells of freedom."

Jane stayed hidden in the branches, unde-
tected, with her hand pressed to the bark.

"Aye, freedom from your proper Cait,"
Raibeart answered, his voice coming through the
dark where he'd disappeared into the trees.

"Murdoch, stop him before he reaches town.
Cait will not teleport ya out of jail again," a third
man yelled, not running quite so fast. "Raibeart,
ya are goin' the wrong way!"

"Och, Angus, my Cait canna live without me,"
Murdoch, the second streaker, answered. "She'll
always come to my rescue."

"I said stop him, Murdoch, we're new to this
place." Angus skidded to a stop and lifted his jaw
as if sensing he was being watched. He looked in
her direction and instantly covered his manhood
as his eyes caught Jane's shocked face in the tree
limbs. "Oh, lassie."

"Oh, naked man," Jane teased before she
could stop herself.

"That I am," Angus answered, "but there is an
explanation for it."

"I don't think some things need to be
explained," Jane said.

"Fergus, Angus, Murdoch, turn it around and
call a meeting at once," Raibeart shouted. "Something foul is afoot. Someone stole the water right
off our land. The stream is not where I left it."

"Raibeart stop ranting, ya drunkard, we have company," Angus ordered. The shadows on his face shifted as he gave a sheepish grin. It was then she saw the similarities to Iain in his features.

"I'm ready, brother. I thought I smelled a *bean nighe* in the forest," Raibeart appeared suddenly, almost too suddenly from where his voice had echoed from. His arms were raised as if he was ready to ward off whatever danger he might face. "Where is that devil's harlot? I'm not scared of death!"

"Cover your bits," Angus muttered.

Raibeart looked at Angus in confusion, then at Jane. He stood frozen with his arms in the air. He sniffed in her direction. "She smells somewhat like a *bean nighe*, but she does not look like one. What kind of fight is this? She's a wee slip of a lassie and far too young."

Jane tried to subtly sniff her arm. She smelled a little like garden soil.

"Raibeart, some decency," Angus scolded.

"Why? I'm not ashamed." Raibeart obeyed despite his words and cupped his hands over his exposed manhood. It became clearer with each passing second that the men had been drinking heavily. To Jane, he said, "Come out of hiding. Ya do no' look like a *bean nighe*. What are ya doin' trespassing in the MacGregor forest in the middle of the night? Are ya a *wulver*? A *shellycoat*? I have a nephew who's a *wulver*."

"The MacGregor forest is that way." Jane stepped away from the tree and pointed toward the direction the men had originally come from. She purposefully kept her eyes averted from their naked bodies. When she looked directly at them, it was only at their faces. "And he's right. You're going the wrong way if you want to reach the stream."

"Where's that *bean nighe*?" Though he had streaked past rather quickly, she recognized Murdoch. He stopped, covered himself and eyed her. "Ya don't look like a *bean nighe*."

"I don't think I am one." Jane didn't stop to consider her strange situation—standing in the woods in the middle of the night, talking to middle-aged naked MacGregors. Even with hands up ready to fight the men looked fairly harmless. Nothing about them set off warning bells.

"How can ya be certain?" Murdoch challenged.

"Pretty sure I'd know if I was a *bean nighe*. I think my dad might have mentioned it to me at some point growing up if I wasn't human. Besides —", she pointed over at Murdoch, "—he said that even though I smell bad, I am too young."

"Not bad," Raibeart corrected. "Just like ya have been swinging through the trees."

"No. I don't swing through trees," Jane assured them.

"Don't suppose you've seen an old washer-woman around here, have ya? Scrubbing away at some old clothes?" Raibeart inquired.

How did he know what she'd hallucinated?

"Quiet now. Don't scare the girl," Angus scolded.

"Don't worry," Raibeart soothed. "The old woman won't want anything to do with ya. And if ya see her, look away quickly and just leave her be. Nothing but heartache there."

"It's just a myth," Angus insisted, gritting his teeth as he gave Raibeart a look of warning. "He's an idiot."

"Nothing wrong with drinking every once and a while and blowing off steam," Jane answered in mild defense of Raibeart.

"Och, no, lassie, he's always an idiot," Murdoch assured her.

Raibeart grinned. "If she's not a *shellycoat*, can I keep her?"

"Sorry, I'm not really looking for a serious commitment right now." Jane gave a small laugh.

"It's settled. I'm marrying this one." Raibeart winked at her. "As long as she's not a *wulver*. Hairy

buggers always clogging up the shower drain—
hey, where's Fergus? We lost Fergus."

"He's trying to resurrect his, um, find
Elspeth," Angus said.

"You're bleeding, Shelly." Murdoch nodded at
her hand.

Jane lifted her hand. Blood had trailed down
her fingers from the cut.

"Ya come home with us. My Cait will fix ya
up," Murdoch insisted.

"Oh, no, it's just a scratch. I'm fine," Jane
tried to step back but her foot hit a rotted limb,
and she stumbled.

"She makes a salve that will leave nary a scar."
Clearly not taking no for an answer, he gestured
his head for her to walk. "Best keep to the front of
us being as you're the only one dressed."

"I'm not sure I'm welcome at your home,"
Jane said. "A woman—"

"Nonsense! Don't be scared, Shelly, I'll lead
the way. And don't worry. We lock the crazy ones
up at night. You're safe with us." Raibeart
charged forward, arm in the air as if leading an
army to battle with his invisible sword. His naked
ass disappeared into the trees.

"He's going to get lost again," Angus said.
"Well, go on, follow the bright light reflecting off
his arse like a beacon."

Curiosity and a sense of adventure caused her to follow. If anything, she'd make sure her neighbors made it home all right. Raibeart had moved too far ahead to see, but she did catch his occasional shout. The two others followed behind her, letting her set the pace.

"What is a *bean nighe*?" she asked, resisting the urge to glance back.

"I think a banshee is what ya kids are calling them nowadays," Murdoch said. "It's a death omen if ya see her washing burial clothes. We call her the washerwoman because of it, a *bean nighe*."

Sorrow filled Jane. She had seen such a woman. If she believed in ghosts because she saw them with her own eyes, how hard was it to believe she'd somehow seen a banshee? The children ghost had indicated her time was near and the *bean nighe* appearing seemed to collaborate it. Not to mention Sean had showed up. That couldn't be a good sign any way she looked at it— even if it was to tell her Dana was dead.

"Stuff and nonsense," Angus inserted. "Just us superstitious Scots. Pay no mind to it. We see signs in everything."

"Oh, I don't know," Jane put forth. "I think all manner of things are possible."

The sounds of Gaelic singing resounded over the forest, coming from Raibeart.

"For example?" Angus inquired.

"Ghosts," she said, not knowing why she did.

"Every house in Scotland has a ghost," Murdoch answered. "And if it doesn't, the English live there and the ghosts don't want anything to do with them."

"What are ya talking about?" Angus snorted.

"I don't know. I'm drunk." Murdoch laughed.

A sound of a scuffle sounded from Raibeart, followed by the rustling of leaves and several large crashes.

"Is he all right?" Jane asked.

"Oh, sure, probably losing a fight against a squirrel," Angus said.

"Or his shadow," Murdoch added. Neither man seemed too worried.

Since Raibeart had wandered off course, Jane led the way to the mansion. The overgrown path opened up to the side yard of the house. Down the hill in the valley, the town lights shone, far enough to create a beautiful pattern of star dust on Earth, but close enough some general shapes could still be made out, like the line of Main Street and the curve of side roads.

Spotlights shone against the siding of the Georgian mansion. The stark white practically glowed against the darker night of the surrounding landscape. From town, it would look like a beacon on the hill.

"How did you get the home painted so quickly?" she asked, furrowing her brow. It was a change she had not noticed when the old lady chased her out earlier. She'd probably only imagined the yellowed paint in her efforts to run away.

"Oh, ah," Angus began.

"Magick!" Raibeart announced, charging from the tree line to the front door of the house. Pieces of forest litter were tangled in his hair. "We cast a spell."

Jane laughed.

"There are a lot of us MacGregors," Angus said, by way of a more reasonable explanation.

"Let's get your hand cleaned up," Murdoch motioned that she should go in.

Well, she'd followed the crazy train this far. Jane stepped into the reception hall. "You have been working hard on this place. The realtor made it sound like this place was falling down around his ears." She looked around, vaguely recalling the room while having raced through it to get away from Iain. The house had sat empty for so long that she imagined it would have been covered with dust and cobwebs before they moved in. The woodwork looked as if it had been installed yesterday rather than over a hundred years ago. The marble staircase and oak banister were polished to a gleam, uncracked by time and abuse. The wide tread had a red carpet down the middle to create traction. Otherwise, the slick stone would have easily sent people to their death.

She stumbled to a stop in the doorway, hesitated, and then started to back away. Her eyes scanned the open railing of the second floor for the old woman.

"I found a wife!" Raibeart announced, stopping her retreat as he pulled her arm to bring her into the middle of the foyer. Someone closed the door behind her with a heavy thud. "And she's not a *bean nighe*, she just smells like one!"

"Um?" Jane looked around, not seeing who he yelled to.

"Not again." A woman's voice chided from a door to her left. "Does this one know ya exist?"

"Aye, she knows, and she's crazy about me," Raibeart yelled. He grinned and winked at Jane. "Don't listen to her, love. Those others meant nothing to me."

"Oh, well, I—" Jane tried to answer.

"Come meet Shelly," Murdoch said in the direction of the voice. "Shelly, this is my Cait."

"It's actually—" Jane started to correct her name.

A woman appeared through the doorway wearing a cashmere sweater set, tweed skirt, and pearls. She looked like something from a 1950s homemaker magazine with her blonde-brown hair pulled back—though she hardly looked old enough to remember being a housewife during the era. Heck, she hardly looked old enough to be a baby in that era. "By all the stars, put some clothes on!" Cait inhaled sharply. "What must the poor girl think of us?"

"She's not been looking," Murdoch defended. "She's been that shade of red since we came across her in the woods."

"We caught her stealing the water," Raibeart added.

"She didn't steal the water," Angus corrected. "Raibeart got us lost again."

"We scared the poor thing and she cut herself," Murdoch went to his wife. "Would ya mind, my Cait?"

"Find your kilts!" Cait ordered. Then, in a more docile tone, she said, "Come, child, this way. Shield your eyes."

Jane found herself obeying.

"Ya must forgive the old fools," Cait said as she led Jane through the formal dining room to a library. A large window showcased the outside gardens. The woman gestured for Jane to take a seat in one of the oversized leather chairs in front of the fireplace. "Let me see the damage."

"They seem harmless enough." Jane sat and held out her palm. The blood had started to dry.

"It will be nothing at all to get that cleaned up." Cait motioned that Jane should remain seated as she stepped out of the room and then back in. Wherever she'd gone couldn't have been too far. "Oh, they're harmless until they get into the ale. I think all that celebrating they did at the pub earlier with the towns-folk sparked the naked revolution ya were party to."

"There are worse things in this world than streaking through the dark," Jane said.

"That there are," Cait agreed. She lifted Jane's hand and began cleaning the wound. The woman had a gentle touch, so gentle Jane could barely feel it. Suddenly, Cait stopped as a tiny smudge of Jane's blood touched her hand. She rubbed her finger over it as if to smear it away, and then studied Jane. "Right…"

"Excuse me?"

"Ya poor lassie. Ya know a thing or two about those others things, don't ya?"

Jane curled her fingers and pulled her hand away. "I don't know what you mean."

"Ya don't have to be worried. Ya can tell me," Cait said.

"I'm sorry. I'm confused. Tell you what?"

"Who ya really are."

Jane furrowed her brow. Her accent was thick, so perhaps something was being lost in translation? "Who I am? I'm Jane. I'm a landscaper and I run a small nursery."

"And your parents?"

"No longer with us. My father was an engineer. I didn't know my mother."

"Lost her young?" Cait asked.

Jane nodded. That was a polite way of putting it.

"Ya don't know about her?"

"She liked old things," Jane said. She'd found a few of her mother's belongings when she was a teenager. Nothing spectacular though. Her father had never wanted to talk about it. "Antiques."

"Give me a moment." Cait stood and again left the room. She took longer coming back, but when she did she carried two glasses. "Here, drink this fast. It's an old family recipe to help keep away infections."

Cait drank from her own glass as if to show it was harmless.

Jane obeyed. Hard liquor burned a trail down her throat to her stomach. For a second, she couldn't breathe. She opened her mouth.

"That would be why I said fast." Cait chuckled.

Jane managed to gasp, and the fire eased. She had no doubt the five-thousand percent liquor would kill any infection in its path. She gasped several more times.

"I can see by your palm this is not the first time ya have cut yourself." Cait reached to take her hand again and traced one of the old scars. There was no judgment in her tone. Leaning over, she placed her nose close to Jane's wrist. "Ya see death, don't ya?"

"Are you a…" Jane furrowed her brow in confusion. Her head spun a little. "Are you a palm reader?"

"Something like that." Cait traced another scar, appearing completely unconcerned with blood contamination as she concentrated on the lines.

"Is it bad?" Jane asked. She blinked heavily, mesmerized by Cait's tracing finger. "It's coming soon, isn't it?"

"Ya know?" Cait looked up at her. Her blue eyes shone with a combination of concern and pity.

Jane nodded. "Yes. For years now. The doctors have run tests, but they don't know what's wrong with me."

"Doctors?" Cait let go of her hand as if confused.

"Yes, because I've been sick since I was a preteen. The last three years were actually pretty good, so I can't complain."

"There are many times when medical doctors have no use," Cait said after a long moment.

"I suppose," Jane allowed, "although I'm very glad to have them in our society."

Cait again grabbed her hand and said nothing as she finished cleaning and bandaging the wound. When she'd finished, she stood. She opened her mouth to speak when an excited shout interrupted them.

"And she's not a *bean nighe!* She just smells like nature. I like it. We're in love."

"I swear, I did not encourage—" Jane explained.

"Oh, we know," Cait put forth, hurrying for the dining room door. "He is going to wake the house."

Jane followed. How could she not?

"Cait kidnaped her, but I don't care that Shelly stole the water," Raibeart was saying.

"Who cast the drunkard spell on Raibeart again?" a young woman with an English accent demanded.

The answer came by way of snickering laughter. "Don't glare at me, Malina. He shouldn't have gotten into my private liquor supply. I told ya someone was stealing my bottles of the good stuff."

As they came back to the front hall, it was to find the stairs and second-floor railing filled with MacGregors in various states of sleepiness.

"There's my Shelly!" Raibeart spread his arms wide as if he expected her to run to him.

"Jane?"

Her eyes found Iain on the second-floor landing. He wore a pair of plaid cotton pajama pants and nothing else. Taking the stairs barefoot, he came down to greet her.

"I thought ya said your name was Shelly," Murdoch demanded.

"No, Raibeart called me a *shellycoat*," Jane corrected.

Murdoch scratched his beard as if trying to remember if that is what had actually happened.

"Raibeart!" Cait scolded as if such a thing had been an insult.

"Wait a minute…" Raibeart demanded. "You're the Jane? The one Iain is pining over?"

Jane bit her lip at the revelation and glanced at the floor, trying not to smile too widely.

"Uncle!" Iain scolded, looking shocked.

"This is her?" Malina asked. "Euann?"

"Yeah, she's the one," Euann answered, nodding and laughing at some secret joke.

"Well ya do have a crush, laddie," Raibeart said. "Rory told us all about it. He said ya chased her out of the house like an inept schoolboy."

Iain made a small noise.

"And ya..." Raibeart turned his attention to Jane. "Shelly Jane, ya can't very well be dating two of us. Why didn't ya tell me before breaking my heart? Lord of the Manor knows I can't take a lassie from Iain. Poor man is hardly pretty to look at. It wouldn't be a fair contest tempting ya away with my charms."

Suddenly, all of them turned their attention upward and to the left in unison. Jane frowned, not hearing anything that warranted such a display. She swayed on her feet and took a deep breath as the fire liquor churned in her stomach.

"Iain," Cait said in hushed tones. She motioned that he should come toward the dining room.

Iain nodded and took Jane by the elbow to usher her from the front hall. As she passed, Cait touched her cheek and whispered something. Before Jane could ask for a translation, Iain had pulled her from the foyer into the dining room. She heard talking behind them but couldn't make out the foreign words.

"What's going on?" Jane whispered.

"I'm trying to keep ya from running again." Iain guided her toward a back door and out into the overgrown gardens.

"Running or being chased off again for being a—what did she call me?"

"It was rude of her. I'm sorry about that. My ma is a little ill right now. Her mind isn't as it should be." He didn't repeat what his ma had said. "She's normally a very lovely woman."

"I'm sorry, it can't be easy having a parent with dementia. When I was younger, I spent some time in the hospital. There was a lady with Alzheimer's who was convinced I was her grand-daughter, Marcy. Every time I was wheeled past Betty's ward, she'd knock on the window and wave at me. It was nice having someone that excited to see me even if it wasn't real." Why was she talking about being sick? She shouldn't be dumping personal information on him. She should be trying to keep a professional distance and not get fired.

"Who is to judge what's real?"

"Her real granddaughter, I suppose." And yet she kept talking as if she couldn't stem the flow of words. "After a couple weeks, I saw Marcy visit, and she wasn't young like me. Betty screamed at her and called her names, not recognizing her for who she was but as some co-worker no one else remembered. That's when I realized what I, in my naivety, thought was cute and harmless was someone else's pain. I guess my point is, I can't be offended by your mother's behavior. For all I know, I'm her grown up Marcy."

"Thank ya for being so kind about it." He caught a lock of her hair as it blew forward and caressed the strands before letting them go back into the breeze.

"I should go. I have a new customer's landscape to plan tomorrow." Jane gave a small laugh before looking around the dark gardens.

"I'm glad ya came back," he said. "And that we had a chance to clear the air about my ma."

"I didn't have much of a choice. Someone had to keep the naked parade from reaching downtown. Sheriff Johnson is a stickler for the law." Jane glanced at Iain's chest and couldn't help but thinking it was too bad he'd not been part of the naked run. That was something she'd like to have seen. "So, what did that woman mean when she said someone cast a spell on your uncle?"

"Oh, ah, Malina? She's my sister." He waved a hand of dismissal. She waited, but he didn't answer her. When she opened her mouth to ask again, he stopped her. "I'm a little jealous that I wasn't with them in the forest tonight. I didn't know there were pretty women wandering around."

"Apparently, I moonlight as a *shellycoat*," Jane said.

"Do ya now?" Iain chuckled and stepped closer to her. She was all too aware of the heat coming off his body. Moonlight caressed his skin, turning it a shadowed blue. The memory of his kiss kept her where she was. "I don't believe it. I think ya would make a better wood nymph than a *shellycoat*."

"That is either very sweet or very strange," she whispered.

"Go with sweet." A half smile curled on his lips as he leaned in for a kiss.

She lifted her hand automatically, and he pressed his chest into it. The steady beat of his heart thumped against her fingers. With it came a drumming in her ears. Iain disappeared, and the garden lit with a bright light.

"Try to run, but do not fuss. We like it when you play with us." The child spirits from earlier giggled.

"No," Jane said. She couldn't see the girls, but she felt them all around her.

"If you choose to stay with him," one said.

"We can keep him in the end," the other finished.

"No?" Iain asked. The bright light instantly went away. He took a step back. "I'm sorry. I didn't mean to presume. I—"

"I have to go." She kept her hand lifted as she backed away.

"Jane—"

"Goodnight, Mr. MacGregor. I'll have some ideas put together for you tomorrow after the farmers market."

"Jane, wait—"

Jane ran from the garden to the side yard, taking the long way home to avoid the forest.

Chapter Nine

"You are a hard woman to track down." Sean lifted a tomato from the market table and bounced it in his hand. There was no place she could run. "If I didn't know better, I would say you were avoiding me."

Jane had seen Sean coming long before he parked along the side of the country road. His shiny black car with silver trim didn't fit into Green Vallis, just as its owner didn't fit into her life. Her stepbrother was charming and beautiful with the attitude of a rock star facing his crowd.

Sean turned his tomato-filled hand and pointed at her to punctuate his words. "You're not trying to avoid me, are you?"

She glanced at his car, wondering how expensive it was. "No. I have a lot of work commitments. Bills don't pay themselves."

He followed her eyes. "Yes. It's too bad your inheritance went to paying off your father's estate."

The statement was sadly laughable. The last time she checked, Dana's spa vacations had not been part of paying off her father's estate. It didn't matter now. Dana was dead. The past was the past. If she made life completely uninteresting, Sean would become bored and move on.

"What will it take to get you to join me for dinner?" Sean continued. "It was your idea after all."

Jane started to speak, but a nearby figure caught her attention. She had never thought she'd be so grateful to see Mrs. Callister. The woman absentmindedly put produce into her basket while staring up at Sean. With each second, the woman inched closer to the man.

"Making a sauce?" Jane asked the busybody.

It took a moment for the realization to dawn on Mrs. Callister. She glanced at her basket full of tomatoes and frowned as if she hadn't realized what she was doing. She set it down and pushed it toward the wooden crates Jane had on the table. "I can never stress enough the importance of setting a nice display even if it's just vegetables." She made a show of rearranging a few tomatoes, setting them on the table around the crates in a haphazard fashion.

"So true," Sean said.

"Fruit," Jane mumbled.

"Excuse me?" Mrs. Callister frowned at her.

"Scientifically speaking, tomatoes are a fruit because they are ripened ovaries with seeds." Jane reached for the tomato decorations and placed them back into the crates. Of course, if Mrs. Callister had called them fruit, she would have argued that culinarily speaking chefs recognized it as a vegetable because it was used for savory dishes. The ole busybody shut her mouth. Jane took the small victory...well, until Sean took it away from her.

"My apologies, Jane, but I agree with this lovely lady here. They are legally vegetables," Sean said, smiling his charming smile at Mrs. Callister. "The Supreme Court ruled on the matter at the end of the nineteenth century."

"I heard that," Mrs. Callister said, clearly lying. She gave Jane a superior look. "Which is why I always say vegetable. Without law, we'd be uncivilized barbarians."

"Excuse me." Jane walked away to help other customers. Let Mrs. Callister and Sean start their little twisted self-loving romance. She didn't have to watch it unfold.

When she glanced back around, Sean was handing Mrs. Callister the basket full of tomatoes without taking payment for them. The woman beamed as she hurried away with Jane's merchandise. "Thank you, young man. Such fine manners."

"Hey, what, no, wait," Jane finished her transaction with the customer and made a move to stop the thievery. The last thing she wanted was for Mrs. Callister to think she was getting freebies from Jane's business.

"Ah, let her be, Jane, they're only tomatoes. I told her I'd take care of the bill." Sean bit into the vegetable-fruit he held. "Mm, these are good. You should be a farmer." Before she could answer, he winked at her. "I'll pick you up tonight at six. Wear something—" he gestured at her old jeans and T-shirt, "—not this."

"I can't. I have an important job starting tonight. I'm landscaping for—"

"You're so adorable, Jane. Planting flowers can wait. We're family. I'll pick you up at six." Sean left without paying.

Jane pressed her hands flat on the table, lowered her head to stare at her dusty boots, and took a deep breath. She didn't want to go to dinner with Sean, but how could she say no? Her father had wanted her to get along with her step-brother. He'd tried to teach her the importance of family—even if you didn't always like them, they were yours regardless.

"You don't look like a *bean nighe*."

Now what?

Jane frowned and slowly lifted her head. Malina MacGregor made a show of giving her a long once over. Jane found herself straightening and self-consciously smoothing out her T-shirt.

What is with today's fashion police? she thought. *Heaven forbid, I didn't dress up for the freaking farmers market.*

Where Jane's nails were trimmed short, and her hands had calluses from hard work, Malina appeared to be a designer-clad princess. Jane's hair was pulled back, more of an afterthought than a fashion statement. White, almost silvery streaks through dark hair framed Malina's face. Jane wore a little makeup, mostly out of the habit to hide any signs of being sick. Malina looked as if she employed an entire team of stylists.

"But Aunt Cait was right. You do have an aura about you." Even Malina's softly accented voice was perfect. "Though I pried, she didn't tell me much, and I had to check you out for myself."

Jane touched her hand. The cut had healed completely. "I didn't have a chance to thank her."

Malina placed her finger on a tomato and ran the tip over the skin of the plump fruit. "How did you do it?"

"What?" Jane furrowed her brow in confusion. She watched the woman's finger. "I guess I just have a gift for gardens. Plants I understand."

Malina gave a small laugh. "You know what I mean."

"No," Jane shook her head. "I really don't. Is this about my receiving your family's landscaping job? Iain hired me because I'm assuming he talked to people and learned I'm very good at what I do. That's how I *did it*. But not to worry. When he hired me, he mentioned you all would have some input into the plans. I'm not sure what the problem is, but nothing has been finalized. We're going to go over everything later today."

"You don't know what I mean." Malina hummed thoughtfully. She motioned to the table. "I'll need all these." Reaching into her small clutch, she pulled out several bills and placed them on the table. "Would you mind bringing them with you when you come tonight?"

"Oh, ah, that will be," Jane reached for the money and started to mentally calculate the total due.

"Keep the change. Call it a delivery fee." Malina smiled and pulled sunglasses off the top of her head. She winked before sliding them over her eyes.

Jane glanced down at the bills and protested, "But this is three hundred dollars. I can't—"

Malina was gone. Jane leaned forward to look down the row of tables to the other booths but couldn't see her.

"Thank you," Jane said, knowing the woman couldn't hear her.

"WHAT'S THIS, LITTLE JANE?" The *bean nighe* did not appreciate the new hint of magick sticking to her human like mold to aging bread. And like mold, it would have to be cut off before the rest could be consumed. "What potions have you been drinking?"

She tried to focus her attention on the country market, but the call of a nearby cemetery kept distracting her. Old death was often the most potent. Those were the spirits that lingered the longest.

Hunger gnawed at her insides, slowly ripping her apart. Oh, what she wouldn't give for a nice passenger train crash, confused souls just ready to be eaten and still full of fresh, delicious emotions. New ghosts were harder to find because the spirits did not call to her like old, musty death.

Sanity was hard for the *bean nighe* to hold on to. Picking off her meals one by one, ghost by ghost, meant she'd only be conscious for short periods at a time before instinct took over. She had to feast upon a big tragedy to sustain any real length of sanity, but even then the hunger would find her eventually. It always found her.

The *bean nighe* knew she needed to feed soon. Unable to handle the pull of the dead, she covered her ears and screeched. Her body sped through the trees, from limb to limb, moving without the direction of her consciousness. She stopped in the middle of a forgotten sunken grave-yard. The weathered gravestones were hidden by weeds, except for a few stubborn markers that poked through in chipped defiance.

An unaware ghost leaned over a divot in the earth, a tomb long forgotten as she mourned a dead loved one. The wailing of the spectral's cries were needles to the *bean nighe's* ears. With mindless purpose, the *bean nighe* endeavored to feed. The unsuspecting spirit didn't even fight her fate.

It started as a tingle in the *bean nighe's* narrow lips, pulling the translucent mist of the ghost's form. Against her will, she absorbed the lost soul, the bitter taste of ghostly pain choking down an unwilling throat. She hated this fate, this burning need to absorb death in order to live. If she denied it, her body forced her to do it. The wailing grew louder because it rang inside her head. So much pain was locked in that ghost's residual moment. The *bean nighe* gagged and convulsed.

When she again had control over her functions, she went to where the ghost had been kneeling and lifted the clothes left behind. They weren't real clothes, but the residual leftovers the *bean nighe* could not consume that looked like the dead's clothing. A new compulsion overtook her and she screeched as she moved through the forest to the little stream. There she would remain, scrubbing and washing the ghost clothing in the water until they dissipated, no matter how long it took. Cleaning up the dead was her one purpose. It was a purpose she longed to end.

"*Salach, salach,*" the *bean nighe* whispered, the word keeping time with the scrubbing on the washboard she'd materialized. "*Salach, salach, salach…*"

Chapter Ten

"I want to help," Rory said, eyeing Jane through the window as she kneeled on the ground and dug small holes. They weren't sure what she was doing, but her backside was pointed in their direction. He grinned at his cousins. "I am suddenly feeling the need to get dirty."

"Me too. Anything the lady commands," Euann added, muscling Rory out of the way so he could get a good look at the woman's ass. "Those stones she was talking about might be heavy. I'm sure she could use a little manpower."

"It will be welcome exercise," Niall added gruffly, his way of saying he was offering his services. He didn't move from his chair or look up from his book. "She should be watched."

"Watched? Ya are a strange one, brother," Euann told Niall.

"She's human," Niall said by way of a dismissive answer, "and there is something off about her. Ma does not like her, and Aunt Cait has concerns. That is enough reason for me."

"Ma is not right in the head," Euann stated. "And Aunt Cait has concerns about all outsiders. Do ya remember what she did the first time she encountered a pizza delivery boy? Poor kid peed himself."

"To be fair, he could have been carrying Pandora's box. No one remembers what it looks like," Niall defended.

"It's a jar, not a box," Euann said.

Niall waved a dismissing hand and kept reading.

"Jane smells like honey," Rory whispered. "Have ya noticed?"

"And I sting like a bee." Euann's voice dipped playfully.

Iain growled in warning. They turned to where he was petrified into a living statue, frozen while walking through the door. It was a weak spell, but enough to force him to listen to their banter without being able to retort...or punch. Rory and Euann had hit him with it mainly out of boredom. While Iain watched, unable to react, they had been spying on Jane. He focused all his energy on trying to shake off the stiffness in his limbs.

"Should we worry? He's starting to thaw out." Rory chuckled, clearly not concerned.

Just then, Iain pushed out of the spell and came flying toward them. Niall shifted his feet out of the way and kept reading, unconcerned. Rory jumped to the side. Iain's unstable aim missed Euann's face and instead hit his shoulder with enough force to send him sprawling.

Euann laughed even as he tumbled to the floor. From his place on the ground, he said, "Easy, queen bee, no one is dipping in your honey pot."

"Unless she asks us to," Rory corrected.

Iain spun a little too quickly, and his vision momentarily blurred as he attempted to shake off the remnants of his family's prank.

"She does make a man warm and tingly to be around her," Euann agreed, not bothering to stand back up.

Iain glared down at him. He didn't want anyone's warm tinglies around his Jane.

"She smells like nature," Niall stated, his tone even as he walked out the back door to go to the gardens. "Most green witch types do."

"Hey, uh, Iain, ya might want to clean that

drool off your chin before going out there. I think your mouth might still be frozen." Euann pushed to his feet as he made his way out the door after Niall.

"Don't leave me alone with him," Rory called, his way outside blocked by Iain. He held up his hands and took a step back. "Iain, don't make me tell Aunt Margareta that ya are consorting with the *reipseach* again."

"Don't ya call her that!" Iain lunged at his cousin. His voice sounded strange since his throat was still a little frozen.

Rory laughed and ran through the doorway leading deeper into the house. Wiping his mouth, Iain sighed in frustration. He should have known the second Jane appeared his family would spring into mischievous action. Now that Erik and Lydia were to be married, his relatives needed something else to occupy their time. The fact Raibeart kept bemoaning his lost love, Shelly Jane, and warning Iain he'd be waiting to reclaim her should his nephew mess things up, didn't help. The ensuing jokes had only stirred the MacGregor clan's need to misbehave.

His feet felt sluggish as he made a move to follow his brothers outside. The sound of Jane's voice drifted over him, and he paused to look at her through the window. Niall stood, arms over his chest, listening to her speak with the countenance of a surly sea captain about to throw a sailor overboard. Euann distracted her by moving his arms to encompass nearby trees and bushes. When Jane turned her back on him, Euann grinned and winked audaciously toward where Iain watched. Rory suddenly appeared, having run the long way around the side of the house.

Iain had seen enough. Slightly paralyzed or not, he wasn't going to leave Jane alone with them any longer.

JANE DIDN'T KNOW what to make of the sudden offers of help. Three MacGregors surrounded her. Rory merely grinned at her to the point she wondered if she had something on her face. Euann smiled and asked an extraordinary amount of questions about trees. As kind as Euann was, he couldn't counteract the severity of Niall, who studied her like he contemplated grabbing a shotgun and running her off the property.

"And ya will work exclusively for us until the job is finished?" Niall asked. He wore a kilt that looked as if it had seen better days. Both it and the loose white shirt were clean, but he clearly didn't put much thought into getting dressed in the morning. It was a trait made all the more noticeable when contrasted to the more immaculate dress of his siblings and cousin.

"Um, well, no," Jane said. "I have other commitments in town. But I will provide you with—"

"Ya smell pretty," Rory said.

"Uh, thank you," Jane answered distractedly before turning back to Niall. "I'll work nonstop until your job is finished. I have extra help who I hire for the bigger jobs so—"

"No rush," Euann insisted with a playful grin.

"There is no need to hire help. We will assist ya," Niall stated. He absently rolled up the sleeves of his shirt. "Tell us what ya need done."

Jane glanced around. Afternoon had turned to evening. "It will depend on what plan you agree on. Perhaps you should speak with Iain and decide what you want done as a family and then I can give you quotes—"

"We're not worried about cost," Rory said.

"I'm sure ya will be fair, lassie," Euann added.

"The sooner we start, the sooner we will finish," Niall said.

You mean the sooner you will be rid of me on your property, Jane thought.

"Forgive Niall the Neanderthal." Euann

dismissed his brother's surliness with an unconcerned wave of his hand. "He hates everyone."

"I do not hate—" Niall began.

"Get off me, hell spawn!" Iain burst through
the doors with his sister clinging to his back.

Jane gasped. Niall sighed and crossed his arms
over his chest. Rory and Euann simply laughed.
No one went to break up the fight.

"Get off me!" Iain spun in circles as Malina
kept her arms wrapped around his head. When
this didn't dislodge her, he finally stopped and
jerked back and forth to try to throw her off.

"You can't go out ther…" Malina's words
trailed off as her eyes met Jane's. She smiled
widely even as she was bounced. "Hi…Jane. Did
you…bring my…tomatoes?"

Jane nodded. Iain's peeked out at her through
his sister's hold. The whole clan of them was
crazy, but at least this crazy batch had clothes on.

"Lovely," Malina said as if her position was
the most natural in the world.

"They're in my truck," Jane answered
belatedly.

"Malina," Iain insisted with a shake of his
body.

"Oh, right." She let go and quickly backed
away from her brother. "Boys, help me carry in
the vegetables." When Malina passed by Jane, she

paused and said, "Sorry about his face. I tried to keep him inside."

Jane frowned in confusion as she was left alone with Iain.

"I'm sorry ya had to deal with my family. I was running late," Iain said.

"No, it's," Jane turned and stiffened, "*omigod*."

Iain's facial skin resembled something akin to a plastic doll that had been smacked on the ground a few times. He looked incapable of blinking, and she was pretty sure the right side of his mouth didn't close all the way as if the lip had been frozen mid-speech. There was very little movement to the underlying muscles.

"It's, ah, it's…" She tried to remember what she was going to say, but it didn't readily come to her.

Was that how all the MacGregors looked so young? They had a great surgeon who made house calls?

"Did you have…?" Jane realized she was unconsciously touching her own temple and lowered her hand. "I mean, you're a handsome man, Iain. I don't think you need to inject yourself with paralytic drugs to…" She made a weak noise. "There's no need to resort to plastic surgery."

He made a sound that was very much like a

nervous laugh as he touched his face. "Right. Plastic surgery."

Jane averted her eyes down his black cashmere shirt and nicely fitted denim jeans. The curve where his hip met his waist caught her attention. Her heartbeat quickened. "I'm sorry, that sounded judgey. I didn't mean it to. It's your body. You can do whatever you want with it. I should stick to landscaping." She forced her gaze to the overgrown path and lifted her arms. "As I was telling your family, it might be best to start closest to the house and work outward."

"So ya think I'm handsome?" Iain asked. She could tell he was trying to smile at her, but somehow the usual devil-may-care was lost in the paralytic effect. Knowing how handsome he normally was, the strangeness was a little difficult to look at—like a 1980s horror movie's special effects gone wrong.

Gone way wrong.

Way, way, *way* wrong.

Even so, that didn't diminish her attraction to him. Her feelings were based on much more than appearance. People didn't look sexy and glamorous every day of their real lives. Jane should know. Most of the time, she was covered in dirt and wore old clothes.

"I think all of you like to say things that will

fluster me," Jane answered. She tried to turn the conversation back to the job. "If we pull weeds from the stones, the paths can be cleaned up fairly easily. Where the paths dip and become too uneven, we can pull the stones and re-lay them."

A hand brushed the back of her arm. Iain whispered, "You're talking fast. Do we make ya nervous, Jane?"

"No." Jane shook her head. It wasn't a complete lie. Euann and Rory were harmless man-boys. Niall frightened her. The elders were mostly a bunch of naked mischief-makers. Only Iain made her nervous—the way he was touching her, the way he whispered her name, the way she wanted to turn and kiss him. She glanced toward the house, wondering if his mother would appear to screech at her again. Not as confident as before, she continued, "Then it is a matter of clearing out the unwanted overgrowth. Once that stage is complete, you will have a better idea of what we're working with."

"I'm sorry we were interrupted." Iain ran a finger along the side of her neck. It didn't take a genius to figure out what he referred to. "And I know my family can be overwhelming. Let us make it up to ya. Stay for dinner tonight."

"You want to make it up to me by having me spend more time with your overwhelming family?" Jane gave a small laugh. "I'm not sure that's a great idea. You're my boss."

"Now that's a game I'm willing to play, lassie." He glided his finger over her shoulder and down her arm. Jane shivered. "Though I think we both know women will always rule over their men."

The possessiveness of his statement caused sadness to well in her chest. She tried to step away. "We should keep things professional."

"What fun is there in that?"

"Iain—"

"Stay," he insisted.

"Iain—"

"For dinner. Stay for dinner," he said. "Ma is feeling better. She'll behave."

"I don't know—"

"Ya will make Uncle Raibeart very happy." Iain grinned.

She tried to keep a serious face but couldn't help the laugh that escaped her. "Are you sure it won't be too painful for him after our failed engagement?"

"I'm taking that as ya are coming," Iain said. "It's settled. Ya finish up what ya need to and come inside. I'll be sure they set an extra place at the table."

Chapter Eleven

"Who is this?" Raibeart pushed up from a mahogany dining table and looked over Jane with a scowl. She would have sworn the furniture looked different from what she'd walked by hours before. Fine porcelain china place settings had been laid out on the shiny surface, complete with cloth napkins, wine glasses, and polished silver. The MacGregors even dined stylishly, like they lived inside a magazine spread. "Iain, what are ya doing with this woman?"

Jane started to laugh before she realized Raibeart appeared very serious. Iain's arm was threaded through hers as he led her into the dining room. She recognized Angus, Murdoch, and Cait. At least this time the men wore clothes and appeared sober.

"What are ya doing with this one? Do ya dare spit in the face of love, laddie?" Raibeart shook his finger in warning before continuing to lecture Iain in Gaelic.

"Da?" Iain pleaded, looking at Angus to stop the man's tirade. Iain's features were beginning to soften, and he was returning to his normal-looking self.

"How is the hand?" Cait asked, leaning to look around Raibeart at her.

"Better, thank you," Jane answered. She pulled away from Iain and was instantly sorry for it. There was comfort in his touch. She showed her healed cut to Cait. "Your husband was right. Your cream worked. It didn't even leave a scar."

"Put that hand down. There will be no spell casting here," Raibeart warned as he slapped lightly at Jane's wrist as if she were a child about to plug a hanger into a power outlet. "Who are ya?"

"It's Jane," Jane said.

"What's that to me? I don't know a Jane." Raibeart eyed her suspiciously.

"Um, Shelly?" Jane said.

"Shelly?" Raibeart suddenly smiled. "My Shelly? Why didn't ya say? Sorry, lassie, didn't recognize ya when your face wasn't dancing around my vision. Hey, ya are a sight prettier and less blurry than I remembered ya being."

"Ignore him," Murdoch stated. "Sanity has never been Raibeart's burden to bear."

"Have ya met the clan, Shelly?" Raibeart asked. He waved his hand over his generation. "These are elders. The children are out playing. I'm the king."

"Who are ya calling a child?" Niall entered carrying a large salad bowl topped with wedged tomatoes. He set it on the table. "And, yes, we met the green witch."

"This is the *wulver* I was telling ya about," Raibeart stated, pointing at Niall. "You'd call him a werewolf. Don't get too close. He bites."

Niall's expression didn't change, but Iain stiffened and took her elbow to lead her around to a chair.

"He doesn't look very hairy to me," Jane said. She couldn't tell if Uncle Raibeart was mentally compromised or just a jokester-troublemaker. Perhaps he was a combination of both.

"That's because he waxes." Euann entered and placed several wine bottles on the table. "Everywhere."

"Real metrosexual, our Niall." Rory brought two large baskets of rolls.

Niall grunted. With his rugged appearance and stoic demeanor, he was anything but.

"Behave yourself," Angus warned Raibeart, pulling the man's arm to get him to follow him out of the room. Raibeart's answer was lost in a string of foreign words.

"Let's get the rest from the kitchen," Cait told her husband. They too left.

"Where are Erik and Lydia?" Iain asked.

"He's probably singing show tunes to her or something," Rory answered with a dismissing wave of his hand.

"No. They're with Charlotte," Euann said. "She's not feeling well."

"I hope it's nothing serious," Jane said, taking the seat Iain had pulled out for her. "Maybe I should offer to bring them soup or—"

"No. Malina has gone to help her. It's nothing that soup can cure," Euann said. "She's having memory, uh…with her…broken—"

"Heart," Rory filled in quickly.

All eyes turned to Iain for the briefest of moments as if by an involuntary tell.

Iain stopped mid-gesture as he reached for a nearby bottle of wine. He didn't pick up the bottle. Instead, he took a seat next to her. A pang of jealousy hit her stomach, but she forced it down.

She leaned into him and asked softly, "Am I missing something about you and Charlotte? Do you need to go?"

"No," Euann broke in a little too firmly. "He's fine where he is."

"No," Iain said more calmly. He gave her a small smile that made her heart do little flutters in her chest.

Murdoch and Raibeart returned with decorative bowls and platters of food.

"Why did your brother call me a green witch?" Jane whispered.

"Ya have a green thumb," Iain said. "It means a woman who is good with plants and nature."

"So it wasn't an insult?" Jane clarified.

Iain shook his head in denial. "No. It's not an insult."

"I can walk myself," a woman chided from the other room. "Quit treating me like I'm about to turn to dust."

Murdoch and Raibeart quickly hurried from the dining room.

"What's going on? Why are ya looking at me like that?" the woman's voice continued. Jane imagined someone whispered an answer because the woman then said, "What are ya babbling on about, ya old fool? I always behave myself."

Angus led the source of protest into the dining

room—Iain's mother. Though she still appeared wrinkled and hunched over, there was a new vitality to her features that had not been there before as if the age had melted off her skin. The change struck Jane as much more than a quick plastic surgery injection, and she found herself standing up from the table.

"Jane, this is my ma, Margareta," Iain stood next to her and angled his body as if he'd put himself between Jane and his mother.

"It's nice to meet you," Jane said.

"What is she doing here?" Margareta asked her husband. She shook her head. "I will not have that—"

"Margareta," Cait said loudly, hurrying in with a bowl of potatoes. She passed them off to Angus before taking the upset woman by the arm. "It's all right. We talked about this. Jane is our guest."

"She grew the tomatoes Malina used in the salad," Iain offered, his voice begging his mother to behave.

"My daughter is careless," Margareta muttered. "If we're not careful, Malina will kill us all."

Iain looked as if he would apologize. Jane shook her head and mouthed, "It's all right."

Jane wanted to say something polite to

Margareta, like she looked like she was feeling better, but no manner of phrasing sounded right in her head, so she stayed quiet. The family began helping themselves to the food. Jane followed their lead, passing serving dishes around and putting small portions on her plate. She had the feeling the MacGregor table wasn't normally so quiet.

"Where's the thing?" Raibeart demanded as he grabbed a wine bottle. The voice sounded abnormally loud in the quiet room. "Ah, never mind. Shelly, do ya want to see a trick?" Not giving her a chance to answer, he placed the flat of his hand over the corked top and slowly lifted. The cork came out of the bottle. Grinning, he dropped the cork on the table and poured himself a large glass of merlot.

"How——" Jane began, awed.

"So, Jane," Euann interrupted. "I like the plans ya have for the gardens."

"Thank you," she said. Raibeart stood and leaned over the table to pour wine into her glass. She made a gesture that he should stop. He didn't and filled it nearly to the top.

"Have ya always had a green thumb?" Rory inquired.

Jane nodded. "Ever since I was a child."

"Why——?" Euann asked.

"Stop interrogating her," Iain broke in. He

slipped his hand onto her leg under the table. She wasn't sure if he was showing support or attraction. "Jane is my guest."

"I was only going to ask why she liked plants so much," Euann defended.

"Plants are simple." Jane looked at the tomato slices in her salad. "If you know how to listen, they'll always tell you what they need, and in return they feed us."

When no one answered, she looked up to see all eyes on her. She noticed everyone had taken salad but no one was eating it. In fact, the salad bowls were pushed forward away from their plates.

"Iain, did ya tell her about the putting green?" Niall inquired, his voice gruff.

"We don't need a putting green," Euann countered.

"Iain, did ya tell her about the puttin' green, laddie?" Raibeart asked. "We have to have the puttin' green."

"Jane has it all in hand," Iain assured them.

"We don't need a putting green," Euann repeated.

"Och, ya are not a real MacGregor!" Raibeart declared, leaning forward to poke his fork past Niall toward Euann. Then, to punctuate his point, he stabbed a tomato wedge. "And ya get no say."

Raibeart opened his mouth to bite the tomato.

"No! Don't eat that." Margareta inhaled sharply and waved her hand toward Raibeart from the far side of the table. Blue light shot out of the woman's palm and caused the fork to fly from his fingers, taking the uneaten tomato wedge with it. The silverware hit the wall with force, and the tines stuck in the wood briefly before it dropped to the carpet.

Jane pushed up from the table. The chair tipped over behind her, and she almost tripped on the wooden legs. She closed her eyes briefly and breathed, willing herself not to fall into a full-blown delusion. When she opened her eyes, all hints of the blue light had gone, and she made her way for the door.

"Jane, wait," Iain moved to follow her retreat from the room. "I can explain."

"I can tell when I'm not welcome," Jane said. She looked at Margareta, hurt. "I'm sorry you don't like me. I'm not sure what I did to you, or if you simply don't like me because I'm American, or poor, or—"

"Or trying to kill my son," Margareta muttered.

"Kill?" Jane answered. She grabbed a tomato slice between two fingers and held it. "I don't even use chemical pesticides in my gardens."

"Ya tell her, Shelly," Raibeart cheered. Everyone ignored him.

She turned to Iain. "Thank you for inviting me, but in the future, I think it's best if we keep to a strictly working relationship. I hope this does not affect my employment."

"Of course it won't," Iain said softly.

"Thank you." Jane nodded once and walked with as much dignity as she could from the MacGregor home.

Once the night air hit her, she inhaled deeply, trying to fight the tears that threatened to fall. Logically, she knew it was stupid to get worked up over tomatoes, but they had been her tiny contribution to the meal. Everything she had went into her work. Her plants were part of her, and the rejection she felt was keen.

The message was clear. The tomatoes she grew were not good enough to eat. Iain's family didn't think she was good enough to dine with them. His mother clearly thought Jane wasn't good enough to be with her son.

A cold chill worked over her. "Go away. I'm not in the mood."

Childish giggles rang out around her. Jane moved faster, charging down the side of the hill in the most direct path toward home. She felt the spirits following her. Lydia Barratt's old Victorian came into view. Jane stopped on the edge of the property. The air was decidedly colder, and she could instantly see the reason for the change in temperature. Spirits had gathered around the home, standing on the lawn as if they waited for something.

"Shoo," an older female ghost ordered. Her translucent form glittered when she moved through the spirit crowd. The unusual sparkling came from her emerald green ball gown. "Get off my lawn. Go on now. Get outta here. There's only room for one spirit here, and that's me."

"Gramma Annabelle, what are you doing, you crazy old bat?" Charlotte Carver ran out of the side door of the home. She worked for Lydia's lotion-making business, *Love Potions*. Jane had heard someone mention Charlotte had just moved into the old Victorian as Lydia's roommate. If Annabelle thought this was her house, it must mean she was Lydia's dead grandmother. Continuing after the ghost, Charlotte grumbled, "What are you doing out here?"

Jane didn't move. What had the MacGregors meant when they said Charlotte was sick? The young woman didn't look too heartbroken or ill. The ghosts on the lawn turned toward Charlotte. Jane watched to see if Malina, Lydia or Erik would join them. No one else came.

Jane always thought Charlotte had a bit of a hard edge to her. Maybe Jane only assumed the woman had an attitude because she was so exotically pretty—tanned complexion, dark brown hair, light brown eyes. Or maybe the attitude was because Charlotte had the same secret Jane did. They both were constantly trying not to acknowledge ghosts.

Charlotte chased the sparkling Gramma Annabelle across the yard. She gasped in pain and then hopped onto one foot while holding the injured foot in her hands. The gathered specters surrounded the woman, but Charlotte didn't seem to notice them. Maybe Charlotte wasn't like Jane after all. Charlotte could only see Annabelle.

"Jane the gardener," Annabelle said, catching her spying on them.

Jane quickly averted her eyes.

"Jane?" Charlotte repeated, dropping her foot as she searched the shadows. When her gaze found Jane, she asked, "What are you doing here?"

Jane tried to smile and focus on Charlotte. It was hard with all their undead company. "I didn't mean to startle you. I was taking the shortcut down the hill. The MacGregors hired me to do some work for them."

"Do you see...?" Charlotte looked at Annabelle and then Jane.

"Yes, she sees me," Annabelle said. "There's something interesting about this one. She's glowy."

It was only with years of practice that Jane managed to pretend not to hear the ghost. Annabelle drifted before her face. Jane focused her eyes through her at Charlotte. "Do I see what?"

"Uh, well, a ghost?" Charlotte gave a nervous laugh and again glanced at Annabelle as the ghost drifted away from Jane toward the others.

Jane pretended to look around the yard. She felt the eyes of those gathered on her. The last thing she wanted was for the crowd to follow her home. "No, sorry, I don't see anything out here but us. Though I once saw a white dog running in the shadows and was convinced it was a spirit until it tried to lick me. I'm sure it's nothing to be concerned over. You're probably just seeing shadows."

"I'm sure you're right," Charlotte said.

Seeing the woman's lost expression, Jane almost relented and told the truth. She knew what it was like to be surrounded by the unknown. Even if Charlotte couldn't see her undead crowd, that didn't mean they weren't affecting her. "Do you feel haunted? I know I sometimes feel like there are a hundred people around when I'm all alone."

"No, not a hundred, just one very big pain in the ass," Charlotte muttered.

"Hey," Annabelle protested. "Who are you calling a pain in the ass? I'm only trying to help you and my granddaughter."

"How is jumping inside me and wearing my body as a human suit helping?" Charlotte demanded under her breath. Then, as if catching herself, she said louder to Jane, "So, the MacGregors."

"Yeah." Jane nodded with a long sigh. "The MacGregors."

"I don't get what the big deal is with them," Charlotte said.

"If you saw under their kilts, you would get what the big deal—" Annabelle tried to break in.

"I mean, I'm happy for Lydia." Charlotte talked over the ghost, clearly determined to ignore her. "Erik is a catch to be sure, but the rest of them…" Charlotte gave a delicate shiver. Frowning, she added, "Especially that Niall. There is absolutely nothing redeemable about him."

"He's a little rough around the edges," Jane agreed, trying to be diplomatic.

"Rough? He's a beast. He bought my apartment building and, when I was in the hospital, he had me served with an eviction notice." Charlotte's gaze wandered to the trees beyond the yard.

"I think he likes you," Annabelle said, drawing Charlotte's drifting attention back. "You should wear something pretty and ask him out on a date. Get a feel for what a Scotsman wears under his kilt. And by feel I mean a handful."

Charlotte rolled her eyes.

Jane pretended not to notice. "I'm sorry to hear that, but this is a nice house. Lydia seems like she'd be a fun roommate."

"Yes, it…" Charlotte's voice trailed off, and she again looked at the trees. Her expression fell. "They're out there, you know?"

"Who?" Jane asked. "Erik and Lydia?"

Charlotte's eyes glazed over. "They have a bag. No eyes in the bag. No breath. Only dark. Dark. Basement."

"Charlotte?" Jane hesitated, not wanting to go near the ghosts wandering close to the woman.

"Drink this," Charlotte told Jane, holding out her empty hand. "Choke it down. Choke."

And there was Charlotte's illness. Not a broken heart, just broken.

"It burns when it comes in," Charlotte insisted.

"What burns? What happened?" Jane asked.

"Go," Annabelle ordered. The short

command startled Jane, and she met the ghost's eyes. It was then she realized the grandma ghost had not been fooled by her act for a second. "You'll only confuse her more if you ask questions. I've got this. Her episode will pass once she gets some sleep. It's no wonder. That Malina was poking around in her head again."

"They want to give me a soul, Gramma, and then they'll rip it out," Charlotte mumbled crazily. "I can feel it in my bones, eating, chewing. Crunch. They want to make me forget, but I see what they're doing. I see. They can't have my soul. I hid it where they will never find it."

Jane slowly backed away as Annabelle helped Charlotte inside the house. The ghosts turned to face the home as if to stand vigil. Jane used their distraction as her chance to escape down the side of the hill. The last thing she wanted was to be followed home.

Chapter Twelve

"What do ya think ya are doing?" Iain demanded in anger. He wanted to chase after Jane. Actually, he wanted to shift into bird form so he could fly after her. But knew he needed to deal with his family first. "Never in my life have I been so ashamed of my family."

"We can't trust her," his ma answered. She looked frail and weak, but he knew better. He'd see the power shoot out of her hand. Jane had seen it too. It was careless of his ma to let magick slip in front of an outsider.

Niall sighed and pushed up from the table. "I'll go after her and erase what she saw."

Iain put out his hand. "No. Ya will not touch her."

"Ya know what must be done, son," Angus

said. He placed his hand on his wife's shoulder. "Niall will be gentle, but her memory must be erased."

"So she ends up like Charlotte?" Iain shook his head in denial. "Shall we place the two of them in the garden with Helena—a whole statuary of those we've failed?"

"I have footage of Charlotte standing on her lawn for three hours in the middle of the night, doing nothing but staring at the road." Euann averted his eyes and concentrated a little too hard on his fingertip. "It's like she's forgotten how to do everything."

"Charlotte was different. We took away her trauma. No one should have to live with what happened to her. Time will fill the gaps she's missing," Niall stated. "Charlotte is not Helena."

"Why would ya have footage of Lydia's house?" Cait asked.

"Erik told me to include it in our security," Euann answered.

"We're warlocks," Iain said in exasperation. "We don't need footage. We need instinct, and my instinct says we do not need to erase Jane's memory. She poses no threat to us."

"Are ya sure it's your *instinct* ya are talking about, Iain?" Euann chuckled.

"She is dangerous." Margareta pushed to her feet.

"How?" Iain demanded. "What has she done that is so dangerous?"

"I can't say yet, but I know something is not right. The memories are coming back slowly." Margareta narrowed her eyes at her son. "But my feelings are not wrong. There is death in her, and that death does not have pure intentions."

"I trust her," Iain stated.

"You're spellbound by her," his ma countered. The others stayed abnormally quiet, watching the ensuing argument.

"I'm in love with her!" Iain shouted. He grabbed a tomato slice and shoved it into his mouth. Talking while he chewed, he said, "And she is not trying to kill us."

"Iain—" Margareta reached for him as if she'd make him spit the food out.

Iain dodged the narrow stream of magick aimed at his stomach. It hit the wall behind him with a small pop. He swallowed. "See, I'm fine. No poison. No ill intention. Not even pesticides. The tomato is a tomato. Jane is just Jane. And whether she will still consider me or not after how my family has treated her, I am hers."

"Iain," Cait said, trying to sound soft and reasonable. He knew better. Cait was powerful in her own right. "Your ma is not wrong. There is something off about her life line. It's jagged. I've only seen the mark in those who have beaten death, and never so many on one hand. Either she's a survivor of some horrific circumstance or she's more than she seems."

"No one questioned Erik's choice." Iain took a deep breath. He loved his family, but he knew his feelings for Jane were real. "Why don't ya trust me?"

"Ya need to trust your family," Margareta said.

"I do trust my family," Iain answered, frustrated.

"Iain, there's more. Her hand. The cut I healed was not the first. I think she is working blood magick. Ya know she's a natural green witch because she has a talent for growin' things. Who knows how far those talents go or what she truly cultivates in those gardens of hers. This is your life, laddie. She admitted to being sick as a child. Perhaps someone taught her how to survive—to *really* survive."

Blood magick? Cheating death? Iain didn't want to believe it. He trusted his family, knew them to be powerful and smart, but he felt what he felt. "I know what a spell feels like. What I feel is not a spell."

"What makes ya say you're in love, laddie?" his da asked.

"I feel something when I am near her. I feel her energy. It's like the plants in the garden waiting to feed my powers without asking for anything in return. When I touch her, I hear bagpipes. When I smell her, I feel the wind inside me. Surely that is love? My entire body hums to life. My heart quickens. I'm more powerful. I even froze time with the mere thought of wanting to be with her." Iain wanted desperately to explain. He needed them to understand. He wanted his family to like Jane, to see her how he did—well, not exactly like he did. "And not just a petrifying spell. I froze everything. Even birds. And they did not fall from the sky like stones either. When I'm with her, time stops."

"Could she have amplified your powers on purpose?" his ma asked, though it really wasn't a question. "If ya were spellbound, would ya be able to tell?"

"Ya think ya care for her. Spells can be tricky like that." Cait held out her hands, palms up. A soft glow radiated from her fingertips. "But spells can also bring clarity."

"What do ya mean?" Iain asked.

"A test," Cait said, cupping one hand under

the other. "One simple test that should tell us all we need to know."

"What kind of test?" Iain frowned.

"A potion." A small blue bottle formed in Cait's palm. "Get her to drink it, but make sure she takes the whole thing. I tried a few drops when she arrived with the naked brigade, but it had little effect on her."

Iain understood natural magick, but mixing potions traditionally fell more to the females of his family. "What will it do to her?"

"It will reveal the truth." Cait stepped forward, presenting the bottle for him to take. "The real trick is going to be in getting her to drink it. Usually to work a few drops can be hidden in hard liquor, but this is a whole bottle. Ya are going to have to be creative, Iain."

Iain frowned. He could just imagine what his aunt meant by creative. "I won't force it down her throat."

"I'll do it," Niall said, resignedly. "And I will erase the memory after. It will be done by morning light."

"Just…" Iain held up a hand in warning to his brother. "Stop. Always with the magickal cleanup. You're not force feeding or erasing anyone."

"Someone in this family has to clean up the messes. I don't see ya volunteering to do what must be done," Niall muttered with just a touch of bitterness. He swiped a bottle of unopened wine from the table. "I'll be in the garden. Let me know when my services are required."

"Laddie," Angus said to Iain. "The family needs to know her intentions. If ya do not have the stomach to give her the potion, let one of us handle it for ya. Your ma is rarely—"

Margareta hit her husband on the chest.

"—is *never* mistaken," Angus corrected without missing a beat.

"No. I'll do it." He finally took the bottle from Cait. Better he than his family. Heat radiated against his fingers. "If this is the only way to prove to ya she does not mean us harm, I'll see to it."

"It's the right thing," Angus assured him.

"Remember she needs to drink it all or it won't work," Cait instructed.

"Be ready to fight," his ma warned. "She might not want ya to see what she is hiding."

"I have nothing to fear from Jane." Iain lifted the bottle. "And I will prove it to ya."

"Take care, laddie," Margareta said. "Death wears many faces and does not like to lose."

Chapter Thirteen

"Jane?" Iain knocked on the nursery building's front door. He knew it was late, or early depending on what day you thought it was, but he had to see her. He'd tried to take a walk, to wait for a decent hour, but the potion bottle in his pocket was a hot little reminder of what he was expected to do. Was he bound by a spell? Was his judgment so wrong when he was with her? He trusted his family. Yet what he felt when he stood near Jane was...magickal. Pure magick. Not a spell. Not a trick. Magick—natural, raw, primal. He was sure of it. "Jane, are ya there?"

"Iain?" A sleepy Jane appeared on the other side of the glass door. Her pajama pants and T-shirt were wrinkled, matching her disheveled hair.

She yawned and scratched her hip. "What are you doing here?"

Guilt filled him at the very sight of her. A man did not call upon a lady at this hour. What was he doing? He didn't want to give her the potion. It didn't matter how valid of a point his family made, he trusted Jane. If he were under a spell, he wanted to stay that way—under her complete control.

"I won't hurt ya," he said, desperate that she should know that. "I need to explain what happened. I know ya must be frightened by my ma, but—"

"Iain, what are you doing here?" She reached for the lock, turning the key she'd left in the inside latch. "Did something happen?" She pushed the door open, and a little bell jingled. "Oh, no, you're here to fire me, aren't you? I don't suppose if I apologized for leaving dinner abruptly it would change your mind?"

"I trust ya," Iain said.

"Ah, okay?" She scratched her temple. Her fingers paused on her head, and she instantly began smoothing down the tangled locks as if just realizing how she'd answered the door. "Does that mean I'm not fired?"

He took her hand from her head and held it in his. "Your beauty could make a rose blush."

"Are you…drunk?" Jane frowned and pulled her hand back. "Do you need a couch to pass out on?"

"Please, don't be frightened of me. I'm sure ya have questions. I can give ya answers," Iain said.

"I'm not frightened," Jane answered. "I'm half-asleep and confused."

"I know seeing light shoot from my ma's hand like that must have been very confusing for ya, but it is going to be all right. We MacGregors are just normal people, well, almost normal, well, not normal at all but—"

Jane stiffened. "Wait, you saw the light come from her hand? I didn't hallucinate that? That was real?"

"Aye. Magick is real. We're warlocks," Iain stated.

"Hallucinations and ghosts and now warlocks," she muttered. "Why not?"

"Ghosts?" He glanced over her shoulder but didn't see any spirits around her.

She shook her head in dismissal of his question. "Am I crazy, or did you just say you were a warlock?"

"Aye. I'm a warlock."

"And magick is real?"

"Aye."

"And you're a warlock?"

Iain nodded.

"A magickal warlock?"

"Aye," Iain said. "I'm a magickal warlock."

"And I'm not hallucinating right now."

"I don't believe so."

"And I'm awake?"

"Aye."

This was not the eloquent conversation he'd rehearsed on his way to her house. In fact, though he'd intended to tell her the truth, he hadn't intended to tell her the entire truth—at least not at first. The more she knew, the more Niall would insist on erasing her memory.

She took a couple of deep breaths. "Huh. All right, continue."

Her reaction was highly underwhelming.

"Are ya…in shock?" he wondered out loud.

Jane slowly shook her head in denial and bit her bottom lip in thought. "No. Not really. Why not a warlock? It makes sense in some ways. And I now understand some of the things your uncles have said."

"I'm a warlock. I do magick. Not magic trick magic like they do in Vegas, but the old magick. I…" He released her hand and held his palms together, creating a small electrical ball of energy.

Jane pushed his hands together and glanced

over his shoulder. "Yeah, maybe you should come inside before someone sees that."

She pulled him behind her into the dark nursery store front before locking the door behind them. Without pause, she led the way across the store to an open door. A narrow staircase went upstairs to her apartment. She slid her hand along the rail as went up, giving small pulls with each step as if to help her tired legs move.

"How are ya not terrified right now?" Iain followed her, confused. Even though he wanted her to be comfortable with who he was, he found himself saying, "I mean, I'm a warlock. I can kill ya with a flick of my fingers. I can magickally entrance ya, so ya have no will of your own. I can throw energy balls at ya. I can levitate ya and throw ya out the window. I can—"

Jane laughed. "I don't think you would have come here to tell me you're a warlock if you intended to kill me and wreck my home."

"How are ya not having a panic attack right now?" Iain barely looked around the small apartment except to get the vague impression of homey comforts—older furniture, knitted blankets, woven rugs on unpolished wooden floors. It felt like her. "Do ya not believe me?"

"Would it make you feel better if I had a panic attack?" Jane sat on the couch and suppressed a small yawn. "I mean, it's almost four in the morning and a little early for a panic attack, but I can try to muster up the energy to fake one."

"Have ya met my kind before?" he asked. "Is that why you're not surprised?"

"If you're going to stand here being all shocked by my easy nature, do you mind if I head back to bed? We can resume this in a few hours if you like. I had a long day and more work tomorrow. Unless you are here to fire me, in which case you better make it five hours because I might sleep in."

"No. I want ya to do the gardens if that is still what ya want. They seem to please ya."

"Then I'll be at work tomorrow." She didn't move.

"There is no reason for ya to go without sleep to do them. Sleep in if that is your wish."

Jane gave a small smile at the offer. "Was there anything else?"

His heart beat faster and his breathing deepened. Iain wanted to tell her everything. Instinct told him he could trust her. His heart told him he loved her. But his family's words circled in his head, keeping him from confessing his full feelings. Perhaps that was for the best, as he might scare her away if he moved too fast. What did he know about being in love—really in love? This was new territory for him. If he came on too strong, he might lose her.

Or was this a spell? What if they were right? What if what he was feeling wasn't real?

His heart squeezed in his chest. The very idea caused a wave of pain inside him.

"My family moved here from New York," he said, trying to remember what he'd planned on telling her. Though, at this point there was hardly any reason to ease her in to the truth. She was taking the news of magick better than anyone he'd ever seen.

Iain touched his pocket, feeling the warmth of the potion. Did her lack of reaction mean she'd already known what he was? Should he simply ask her to drink it? Even in his own mind, asking a woman to drink a strange liquid in the middle of the night sounded sketchy.

"I seem to recall hearing that." Jane braced her elbow on the arm of the couch and leaned into her hand. "It's an abrupt segue in conversation, but all right, I'm following."

"We move around a great deal, every twenty years or so. That's quite a bit for us, maybe not for mortals. The city was nice for blending into the crowds, but it lacks nature. That's why we're here. For the nature." Iain placed his hand on his hips but felt too much like a dictator, so he crossed them over his chest. Her steady eyes were on him, watching. Nerves bunched up his stomach and made his limbs tingle.

"So you moved for a change of scenery. I hear city folk do that," she prompted.

Why was she so calm? Iain began to pace. "No, no, we need nature. It fuels our powers. Without it, we wither. Here we can take from the forest as a whole rather than kill a single tree. We live in peace with nature because it gives us life. It's like we plug in to it and…and…light up." Iain let his body glow briefly.

"You're a walking Christmas light?"

"No," he said a little defensively. "I'm a powerful warlock. I've lived for hundreds of years." Realizing he sounded like a petulant child, he dropped his arms to the side and took a deep breath.

That seemed to register with her, and she shifted to a more attentive position on the couch. Finally, a reaction. Now he could ease her into his arms and comfort her fears like he'd first planned.

"You look good for being hundreds of years old," she said.

So much for easing fears. Iain sighed again, louder.

"You were saying, you plug into trees like a light bulb," Jane prompted when he didn't readily continue. "I've heard of potatoes being used to conduct electricity, but never a tree. Please go on. This is all very fascinating."

"I'm not a potato." Why wasn't this conversation going well? Did one of his brothers cast a spell on him to take away all his charm? Euann would think such a thing was hilarious. He took a deep breath, hoping he'd sound more intelligent if he slowed his words. "It's power, not electricity. And it's not always nature. Sexual energy can give a rush though it's more of a surge rather than a steady stream. An orgasmic rush."

Jane pushed up from the couch and stood before him. Bloody hell, the woman was beautiful. And he was an idiot babbling about light bulbs. The soft lamplight caressed her cheek, falling along her neck as she moved. She mesmerized him. She didn't need makeup or glamorous attire. Her messy hair and nighttime clothing were more seductive than anything he'd seen in his life. She was just Jane, simple, perfect Jane.

"Is this a warlock booty call?" Jane's voice brought him back to the conversation. "Did you come over here looking for a little magick surge?"

"What? No." He cleared his throat and shifted uncomfortably to hide his rampantly growing attraction. "I came here to tell ya I trust ya. I'm being very gallant. You're a lady, and I would never presume to—"

"I didn't know my trust was in question."

"I'm not explaining this right." Iain wanted to hold her. With each passing second, the bottle in his pocket became hotter, fueling his guilt over what he was expected to do. "Everything about ya is nature. That's why Niall called ya a green witch."

"Do you think I'm a witch?"

"No, not necessarily a real witch with magick but a woman of nature talented with plants."

"Okay, because I don't have any magickal powers. I just grow things."

He studied her hand. "I think there is more to ya than just growing things."

She gave him a small smile. "I see things."

"What kind of things?"

"I see a potato. Here. Standing before me. Able to light up like a Christmas tree." Jane laughed softly. "What about you? Any special powers?"

"My gift, my power, is to help nature recover after it fuels us. When I'm near ya, I feel more powerful like my own energy is bouncing back at me through ya." He breathed harder, feeling that energy grow between them. "Ya smell like honey."

He closed his eyes. "Your skin feels like flower petals." He reached his hands toward her.

"Iain, what is this all about?" Her voice was soft, gentle. Fingers glided over the backs of his hand, and he trembled at her touch. "If you're worried about what your mother did, don't. I'm relieved that it wasn't a hallucination. I can't always tell if something is real, a hallucination or a ghost trying to play games. Life is too short to live in fear. Well, my life anyway. I don't startle easily, and the idea of warlocks doesn't scare me. You don't scare me, Iain."

He opened his eyes and found her standing close.

"But I think I understand what you're trying to tell me. Your family doesn't trust me. That's why you're here." She nodded sadly. "If I affect you, they must sense it and they naturally become protective of you because they don't know my intentions."

Unable to help himself, he gave a small smile. "Ya have intentions?"

Her eyes dipped, and she released his hands. His skin tingled in protest. She shook her head. "No."

He waited for her to elaborate, but she didn't.

"I wasn't kidding when I said it is too early to

be awake. Are you going to stay?" she asked after a long silence.

"Are ya asking me to stay?"

Jane laughed. "I didn't think coyness was in the MacGregor DNA." She tilted her head, indicating that he should follow. "Come on, Potato."

Iain chuckled at the use of the nickname. "Now, lassie, don't ya be callin' me that in front of anyone."

"What? You don't want your brothers hearing me call you my little sweet potato?" She turned to wink at him.

How could Iain resist following? Wood planks creaked with each step. Her apartment looked nothing like the elegance of the mansion, yet there was a bohemian charm to the faded wallpaper and big square art canvases. Worn paperbacks were piled on side tables. He noticed herbs growing in small pots on the windowsills. With a couple of spells, he could transform her room into a palace, but he didn't want to change a thing. Why change perfection?

Her metal bed frame creaked with age when she climbed onto it. The disheveled bedding blended with her clothing in the dark. The room smelled of honey, luring him to her. Unbidden by his conscious mind, tiny lights danced along his fingers, swirling from the tips into the air like tiny stars to cast a soft light over her features. She looked at him with complete trust, no fear or hesitance in her gaze. The lights moved, surrounding her. She lifted her hand, letting her fingers collide into the starry heaven he'd created for her.

"They tickle," she whispered, giving a small laugh.

If his family could only see what he saw in her, they wouldn't ask him to test her. Iain let his clothes slither from his body, magickally melting into a pile on the floor. Her eyes instantly turned from the dancing lights to him.

"Come here." She reached for him, her smile open and welcoming. "I promise no one is storming in here to interrupt us this time. It's a perk of living alone."

Iain tried to think of something charming to say. After centuries, seduction should be second nature. It should be him seducing her, him coaxing her to his bed, and yet here he was, helpless as a virgin in front of the goddess of temptation.

Iain crawled naked onto the bed, making it bounce in his excited haste. Jane laughed as she slipped and fell back onto the pillows. Her hair spread in loose, wild curls around her head. She lifted a finger to his forehead and brushed his hair aside only to have it fall forward once more.

"Say something," she whispered. It was then he realized he merely stared down at her. His body was tight with desire, that much evident by the straining arousal between his legs. Yet his heart hesitated as if this was a dream he could chase away.

"Ya make me want to freeze time," he answered.

Iain lowered his mouth to hers. The suppleness of her lips again reminded him of the softest petals in nature. She was a flower, in some ways delicate and soft, yet hearty and bold like the heather of his homeland.

Home.

Iain's breath caught, and he had to end the kiss. His magick danced along her cheek in tiny blue sparks. Jane reminded him of home. Not the mansion on the hill, not the endless cityscapes and towns before that, but of his real home—the Scotland of his youth, of the feeling he had standing on the moors, land uncluttered, the air stirring, the people unrushed and unafraid of hard work. It was something from so long ago, sometimes an unclear notion, but still so much a part of him. He'd never thought to find the feeling of home again.

"IAIN?" Jane whispered when he didn't move.

His naked body molded against hers, kept away only by the thin layer of clothing. The material did nothing to protect her from the hard shape of his lines. Where his magick touched, she tingled, sparks lighting her nerve endings like fire lit a slow-burning dynamite fuse.

Relief had filled her when she learned that the power she'd seen shoot out of Margareta's hand was real. She hadn't hallucinated it. She wasn't getting worse. The knowledge gave her hope.

"I want time to stand still," he whispered. "I don't want to lose this moment."

"It is a good moment," she agreed, keeping her words as soft as his. The tiny specks of magick he'd created drifted around them as if to cocoon them from the outside world. She felt safe as if nothing beyond the bedroom could touch her.

"I have to tell ya something."

Jane smiled. She saw the hesitance in him and wondered what had caused the sudden insecurity. "I know. You trust me."

She lifted her head to close the distance between their lips. Iain didn't resist as she kissed him. He instantly deepened the contact. The tingling sensation of his magick infused her lips. Iain's hand traveled between them, down her chest. At first, his fingers moved over material, but suddenly he touched skin. Jane gasped, breaking the kiss to glance down. Her clothes had disappeared.

Iain merely smiled and resumed kissing her. Magick trailed his fingers, heightening her desires. Her legs intertwined his. She explored his body, running her hands over his smooth flesh. His ass flexed, and his hips pushed forward.

The pleasure of his touch caused a euphoric rush through her veins. She felt him pulling emotion from her, a physical tug that left her both weak and helpless. Her hands began to fall from his chest. Iain thrust her energy back, filling her with his very essence. The sudden rush of feeling invigorated her. It was more intimate than a thrust of the body.

"I told ya that ya replenish me," he whispered.

She felt him inside her, connected to her emotions. No words were needed as he instinctively knew how she liked to be touched, kissed, loved. It was an intimacy she had never known before. She felt him more than she felt herself. His magick joined his flesh to hers, tiny blue threads that strung between them. The glow illuminated his handsome face in the dark room.

"Iain," she said, the word shaky. "I-I feel…"

His hips came between her thighs. "Aye, I feel too."

Iain rocked his body against hers. The length of his arousal tingled her sex, rubbing her clit. Jane tensed and jerked as an orgasm racked over her at the stimulation. She gasped noisily for breath.

"Not bad for a Christmas light, huh, lassie?" Iain grinned.

Her heart pounded. All she could manage as an answer was a panting laugh.

Before she'd recovered, he angled his cock to enter her. She moaned. The connection between them grew, this time without magick. He gazed into her eyes, keeping his face close to hers. Nothing existed beyond this moment.

Iain made love to her slowly. The residual magick clung to their skin, shimmering like glitter. He cupped a breast before sliding his hand along her hip and down her leg to hold on to the back of her thigh. Pleasure built naturally between them until she couldn't hold back any longer. She came, her body clutching his. Iain stiffened, and his eyes changed. The pupils become wide as he climaxed and then returned to their normal size.

He dropped his head forward, and the magickal stars dancing around them rained over them. They crashed onto their skin and then faded. The aftermath left her relaxed, and she turned with Iain as he lay down next to her on the bed. Snuggling into his arms, she suppressed a yawn.

"Not bad for a potato," she said, chuckling as she closed her eyes. No part of her wanted to move.

"For ya, love, I will be anything ya want...even a potato."

Chapter Fourteen

Jane's mind awoke, but her eyes remained closed. Iain's naked body curved along her back. Blankets cocooned them. For the first time since she could remember, she didn't care what time it was. She didn't have the need to crawl out of bed to work one of her many jobs. She was in a moment.

One perfect moment.

Sex had been…well, mind-blowing, magick-blasting, toe-curling awesome. But this moment was perfection. Her skin made contact with his skin. His steady breathing stirred her hair. It was a feeling she'd always longed for but until now had never felt. It was exhilarating. It was frightening. It was indefinable.

It was perfect.

"Mm," Iain moaned sleepily. "What are ya thinking about, love? I feel ya radiating onto me."

They lay in silence for a long moment, but the sound of his voice had stimulated her conscious mind.

"I don't want to move," she whispered.

"Then don't move," he answered just as quietly. "Green Vallis is a great town...now that the MacGregors are here."

She gave a small laugh. "That's not what I meant. I don't want to move out of bed."

"I don't want to move out of bed either. Let's live here." His body made small movements as if he snuggled deeper into the mattress.

"Don't you think your family will notice and come looking for you?"

"My brother and cousin will probably come looking for ya."

She stiffened against him. "They don't think highly of me, do they?"

Iain brushed the hair from the back of her neck and kissed her nape. "Just the opposite. If they think I've gone missing, they might get ideas and start to think they have a chance with ya."

Jane smiled at the compliment. "It must be nice having so many people around all the time. You said you move quite a bit? Do you always move together?"

"We're a giant clan of Scots. It's easier to control our magick if we're together. Plus, we're family. Ya don't leave family."

"I don't have a family. Not since my father died." Jane turned in his arms to study his face. She lay next to him, their heads facing each other on the same pillow. "Well, there's Sean, my step-brother, but he's not really my family. I don't even know what he's doing in town. He keeps trying to have dinner with me, and I keep avoiding him. Not really the best way to handle the situation, but he doesn't take no for an answer. I should just go and get it over with. I'm sure he's just here to finalize his mother's affairs. I'm told my step-mother passed away."

"I'm sorry. Were ya close to her?"

"No. I know that makes me sound like a horrible person, especially to someone like you who has such a close connection to your family, but she was an unhappy woman."

"Over the centuries, we have had our moments, but I know I am lucky to have them."

Centuries. The word struck her, and she found herself staring at his chin. He had centuries. She had limited moments. There was no use crying about how unfair life was, but she also didn't have to dwell on the fact.

"What about your mother?" he asked.

"My birth mother left us when I was a baby. I guess she couldn't handle family life. I don't remember her so I can't really miss her. But enough of my poor-me family talk," Jane dismissed, only to add before he could protest the change in conversation, "Since you move around so much, where was your favorite place to live?"

"*Llanfairpwllgwyngyllgogerychwyrndrobwllllantysilio-gogogoch* on the island of Anglesey in Wales," he said, without stopping to consider the answer.

"Did you just have a seizure?"

"No, it's a real place."

"*Lan. Vire…*" Jane gave an unladylike laugh, cutting off her own attempt at repeating what he'd said.

"Would ya prefer the shorter version? *Llanfair-pwllgwyngyll?*"

"You are just making things up. That can't be a real place."

"Technically, I haven't lived there, but it is fun to say." Iain chuckled and drew his finger down the slope of her nose to press it against her lips. "But maybe don't try to speak Welsh. Ya butcher the language."

Jane pretended to pout. "The romantic answer would have been to say *Green Vallis* is your favorite place."

"Mm, this apartment is my favorite place.

Let's never leave it. We'll stay cocooned here in blankets."

"And starve?"

"I can materialize tomatoes out of the garden if ya want, love. All ya have to do is ask…and refuel my magick." He winked and tried to nuzzle her neck.

"*Lan. Vire. Pool…*" she tried to sound out.

"*Llanfairpwllgwyngyllgogerychwyrndrobwllllantysilio-gogogoch,*" he said against her skin.

"Show off!" She playfully hit his arm.

Iain drew a fingertip from the tip of her ear down the slope of her neck. It tingled where he touched, and she knew he was stirring her nerve endings with magick. It wasn't necessary. He didn't need magick to stir her to him.

"Are you hungry?" She closed her eyes and gave a small moan of pleasure. "I can materialize you something un-magickal in the kitchen if you like.

"Only for ya." He brushed his lips over hers.

Jane melted against him. Her heart pounded so hard she heard it knocking in her ears. Wait, no, that wasn't her heart. Was it Iain's?

Iain pulled back. "Are ya expecting company?"

"What?" She tried to lean back into the kiss.

"Someone is at the door." He rolled up from

the bed and reached for his jeans. "Would ya like me to get it?"

"And shock my customers?" Jane asked, slower to get out of bed.

"Either someone is having a tree emergency or…" Iain frowned. "I don't like the sound of that knock. Ya wait here, love. I will handle this."

"Iain, wait—"

He strode from the room naked only to have his clothing materialize on his body as he moved through the doorway. At his use of magick, she felt a tiny pull at her skin as if he'd taken part of her to make it happen. The sensation was weird, but she shook it off as she hurriedly tugged on clean clothes.

"Who are you?" Sean's voice demanded as she rushed down the stairs. "Where's Jane?"

"I think it's time ya took a hint and turned yourself around, laddie," Iain answered, the condescension clear in his tone.

"What? You have no right to speak to me like that," Sean yelled. "Get out of my way."

"She doesn't want to see ya," Iain said. "If she did, she'd have shown up to dinner."

Jane cringed at the blunt statement. Though it was true, she normally tried handling things a little more delicately. She passed through the aisles of her store. The shelves were filled with supplies, but she didn't keep regular shop hours for the public. She grabbed Iain's arm and put herself forcibly in front of him. "Hey, Sean, what's going on?"

Sean's angry eyes stayed focused on Iain for a few seconds before he turned his attention to her. "You did not make it to dinner yesterday. We had plans."

"Yeah, I'm sorry about that." She lifted her arms to gesture that he should go outside, away from Iain. He didn't move. Making a weak noise, she glanced over her shoulder. Iain's narrowed eyes focused on Sean in an expression of what could have easily been perceived as a threat.

"Iain, would you mind giving me a second?"

"I'm fine where I'm at," he said, refusing to give them privacy. "Take as many seconds as ya need."

Jane frowned. "Sean, why don't we go outside?"

"Fine," Sean grumbled. He held the door for her as if to make sure she would go outside with him.

Jane glanced back at Iain in warning and held up her hand to indicate he should not join them. The direction of the sunlight denoted it was late morning. When they were alone, well, as alone as a watchful warlock staring at them through a glass door would allow them to be, Jane said, "I'm sorry I missed dinner. I explained I'm busy with a lot of jobs right now."

"Yeah, *jobs*," he said bitterly, glaring toward the door.

Jane didn't appreciate his tone or his implication. "Sean, don't be crass. I'm allowed to have a personal life. I don't see you for years and then you expect me to drop everything the second you drive into town."

"That's not my fault. You disappeared from our lives. I had to track you down. How was I to know you wouldn't leave before I had a chance to see you? Is it so wrong that I want to spend time with the only family I have left? My little sister?" He reached as if to touch her face but then must have thought better of it, because he ran his fingers through his hair instead.

Just like his mother, he always knew just what to say to guilt her. Knowing it was a lame excuse even before she said it, she answered, "I'm sorry. You're right. I would have called, but I don't have your current number, and besides, my cell phone is broken. I dropped it on a landscaping job and haven't had a chance to replace it."

"You know I am staying at the Dorchester. You could have called there for me."

"I don't have a house phone. Only the broken

cell." She could tell by his look he wasn't impressed with her explanation.

"I don't like that man you're with. There's something off about him," Sean continued.

"We'll have dinner tonight," Jane said. She was not discussing her private life with him.

"Why don't we just go now?"

Jane looked down at her clothes. In her rush, she'd grabbed an old polo shirt and faded blue jeans. Good thing the shirt material was thick, because she wasn't wearing a bra underneath. "I'm not dressed for dinner. I'm not even wearing shoes. Tonight. You have my word."

"Fine. I'll be here—*again*—at seven." Sean tried to come in for a hug, but she artfully stepped back.

Jane nodded. "Yes. Seven. I promise."

Iain opened the door for her as she gingerly stepped barefoot across the lawn. Seconds later, the squeal of car tires blasted over the quiet street.

"I don't like the look of him," Iain said. "Ya are right to be wary."

"Iain, just..." She took a deep breath, trying not to be upset. "Just go."

"But...?" He gave her a confused once-over.

"I can handle my own business," she said. "I don't need you answering my door for me or trying to handle my stepbrother."

He reached for her. "But we're—"

"Having a good time," she inserted.

"I think we both know it's a little more than that, love." He placed his hands on his hips and studied her. She hated the frown on his face and the confusion in his eyes. "As your man, I will protect—"

"We can't be more than that." Jane took a deep breath. "I think you should go. I need to run a few errands before I start the landscaping. I'll be by the mansion later."

"Jane, we need to discuss—"

"Goodbye, Iain," Jane stated. She moved to go upstairs, unsure whether she wanted him to follow her or not. On one hand, she didn't need him swinging in and playing hero. She was a grown woman who could handle her own affairs like she'd been doing her entire adult life. On the other hand, it felt nice to be protected and wanted. Then again, what gave Iain the right to be rude to her stepbrother? Sure, she didn't like Sean and didn't want him in her town, but he was her family, and he was her annoyance to deal with in her own way.

Back and forth, her mind swung like a pendulum. She was mad. She wasn't mad. The only thing she could firmly state was that she was confused.

Chapter Fifteen

Iain made sure to magickally lock Jane's front door before starting the walk back home. He didn't like Sean around her but couldn't fathom if it was for any real reason, or if the possessive, primitive bird of prey shifter inside him didn't like other men sniffing around his territory. Jane might see Sean as some harmless, annoying stepbrother, but Iain wondered if Sean saw Jane as a sister. Sean didn't look at her like a man looked at his sister.

Iain had lived far too long to not trust his instincts, and his instincts said to keep Jane away from Sean. Then again, in all his centuries, Iain had never felt for any woman the way he did for Jane. It was new territory for him. Had possessiveness caused his reaction instead of instinct?

Churning thoughts remained his steady companion as he walked the distance to the mansion on the hill. A few townsfolk stopped to wave at him. Iain vaguely recognized their faces as he automatically returned the greetings. Another town. Another sea of faces. Another step forward in their journey as immortal warlocks. Yet Green Vallis was different than other towns they'd lived in. His magick felt it. His body knew it. His heart understood it. Jane was here. Erik had found Lydia. Power surged from the very ground Iain walked on like a convergence of ley lines.

He paused at the clarity of the thought. If ley lines converged beneath them and somehow created a surge of energy, it would act like a beacon to not only his family, but to others too. It would explain why the *lidércs* had tried to force Charlotte to take his powers from him.

Oh, poor, poor Charlotte. He hoped his magick didn't cause permanent insanity. The more he stayed away from her, the better her chances.

"I'd call this your walk of shame, but if I'd spent the night with a woman like Jane, I'd be bragging about it," Rory said. A shotgun rested over his shoulder as he strolled across the expansive lawn.

"What are ya doing?" Iain frowned.

"Hunting." His cousin grinned. It was the kind of mischievous look that Iain had seen numerous times.

"We don't hunt." Iain stopped walking as Rory joined him. "Put that away before ya rile up the locals."

"I'm not killing anything," Rory dismissed, unconcerned. "Just doing a little target practice on Euann's surveillance cameras."

Iain couldn't help but chuckle. "He's going to retaliate, ya know that, right?"

"Let him." Rory shrugged and continued his leisurely walk to the nearby trees.

Iain was too occupied to interfere, and would probably not have done anything to stop Rory even if he could have. Warlocks would be warlocks, after all.

The second Iain opened the door, his ma and Aunt Cait were waiting for him. They swooped forward like two tigresses on their prey.

"Well?" Margareta demanded. "What happened?"

Iain grimaced and made a move to go toward the stairs. "Since when have I ever discussed my sex life with ya?"

His ma scowled.

"The potion," Cait clarified. "What happened when ya gave her the potion?"

Iain stopped on the bottom stair and stiffened. He reached for his pocket, but the potion bottle wasn't there. "I, uh…"

"Ya slept with the *reipseach?*" Margareta shivered. Each passing hour seemed to bring new vitality to the woman. She looked younger than she had the night before. It meant she was finally recovering from her overuse of magick.

"Ya look better, Ma," Iain said. "Glad to see the rose returning to your cheeks. Maybe next time leave some things to chance. I know ya wanted to help ensure Erik's Lydia was out of harm's way, but ya pushed yourself too far."

"Lydia?" Margareta repeated. Her eyes were clearer too. Her memory was coming back to her. "Ya think it was Lydia's future that sapped me of my strength?"

"That is what ya intended to find out with your future casting, right?" he questioned.

"I'm sure it was something more," Margareta said. "Peeking into the future doesn't cause a person's mind to—"

"The potion?" Cait interrupted. "What happened when ya gave it to her?"

"Nothing," Iain said.

"I told ya to make sure she drinks all of it," Cait scolded. "Ya will have to try again."

"She drank none of it," Iain admitted.

"What?" Margareta shot in ire. "Give it to me. I'll see to it."

"I think it fell out of my pocket at Jane's house last night." Iain slowly backed up the stairs, keeping his eye on his elders. "I said I'll take care of it and I will."

"Ya lost a potion?" Cait demanded as if she couldn't believe such carelessness.

"It's not lost, just misplaced," Iain said. "Jane will be here later to work on the landscaping. I'll retrieve it then."

"That *reipseach* bewitched him," Margareta swore. "That is the only explanation as to why my son would be so careless."

"Jane is not a hussy," Iain stated firmly. "I'll not have ya saying such again. I care for her, and the only spell I'm under is the emotion I feel for her. I told ya I'd take care of the potion and I will."

He hurried up the stairs before he could hear any more of their talk.

WARLOCKS.

The *bean nighe* clung to her branch as she watched the hunter pass beneath her. His eyes turned up, flashing with unmistakable magick before he continued on his way. She wasn't worried. He would not be able to see her now that she'd fed on spirits in the old graveyard. He kept searching the trees as he moved, and seconds after he disappeared, she heard the report of the gun.

What was little Jane doing with warlocks?

The *bean nighe* had followed one of them from Jane's home, not liking the magick she'd been sensing around the woman lately. Now it all made sense. Jane's life was infested with warlocks.

Oh, if only she could feed off one of those immortal souls. Magick and food all in one bite. She would not have to steal fresh souls from the reapers after a tragedy to retain any length of consciousness. With a warlock, she could last years, maybe even decades. Alas, such a meal was merely a dream, for it was rare to find a dead warlock who had not had the clan funeral rites, and she was not strong enough to kill one.

Time was not the *bean nighe*'s ally. Even now, the call of the dead echoed its way to her, stirring the gnawing hunger. Soon she would not be able to resist taking another meal.

Chapter Sixteen

There was familiarity in dirt.

Jane loved the feel of soil on her hands. She liked crumbling clay through her fingers. She recognized and appreciated the potential of earth.

Dirt she understood. Plants she understood. The MacGregors…not so much.

She knew they were warlocks. They knew she knew they were warlocks. And yet they pretended like their secret was still their own as they lifted landscaping supplies off her small trailer and manually carted them across the lawn.

"How did ya do that?" Iain asked.

Jane blinked in confusion, looking up at him from her place in the ground. To be fair, he had tried to talk to her when she first arrived, but she'd still been irritated with him. It was nothing a few hours landscaping couldn't calm. "What?"

"That." He gestured past her.

Jane turned. The nearby bushes had filled out with leaves and looked healthier than before. "It's amazing what a little weeding and water will do."

"That's not weeding and watering," Iain stated. "Those were near dead earlier."

"You exaggerate," she dismissed. "They only look fuller now that I've cleared the area."

Iain kneeled on the ground beside her. He took her dirt-filled hand in his. Her fingers tingled where they touched. "No, it's your doing."

"I have always had a way with plants," she said weakly. "It's no big deal. Just a green thumb."

"Told ya she was some kind of green witch." Niall passed with three heavy stones stacked on his arms. Jane could only manage one of the stones at a time, and even then her steps were stilted from the weight.

She turned her hand, so the dirt poured onto the ground.

"Here. Try digging over here." Iain stood and reached his hand to help her to her feet. He led her to a bush.

Jane kneeled on the ground and began pulling weeds. She took the hand rake from her belt and churned the earth. The more she worked, the better the nearby plants began to look. She paused to examine the leaves.

"I've never seen anything like it," Euann said.

Jane turned in surprised to find Iain, Niall, Euann and Rory forming a half circle around her, watching.

"What are ya?" Rory asked.

"Uh—" Jane gave a small shrug, "—a landscaper?"

"No, what are ya?" Rory repeated. She waited for his playful smile. It didn't come.

Jane stood, not understanding. "I don't know how to answer that."

"Maybe ma was right." Euann gave Iain a pointed look.

"Ya should have given her the potion, Iain," Niall said. "That is the simplest way to have our answers."

"Potion?" Jane took Iain by the arm and pulled him away from the others so they couldn't listen. "Does he mean the pretty blue bottle you left at my house? I thought it was cologne or something. I was going to return it."

Iain nodded. "I was going to explain about that, but we—" he gave her a sheepish grin, "—became distracted last night."

"Explain it now," she said. "Is there a reason

your family doesn't trust me and that you keep trying to reassure me that you do?"

"They think you're trouble." He tried to touch her, but she leaned back, refusing to let him sidetrack her. "Where did ya put the bottle?"

"Locked in my glove box," Jane answered. Her heartbeat quickened. "Why? What does it do? Is it dangerous? Should I not have touched it? Why are you just now telling me this?"

"Jane, easy," he soothed.

"Easy?" she repeated. Why was he so calm? In fact, he always looked calm—unless he was glaring at Sean.

"It's a test of sorts. My family wanted me to give it to ya to drink to see if ya can be trusted." Iain reached for her. "But I trust ya. I don't need a test to tell me—"

"I have to do everything," Niall stated.

"Niall," Iain warned, turning to face his brother.

Niall lifted his hand and a yellow light radiated from his fingertips toward Jane.

Jane felt her feet and legs stiffening, trapped in place against the dirt. She gasped in panic, her eyes finding Iain's as she tried to reach for him. "I can't move."

The last word barely made it out as the petrification seized her chest and throat.

"WHAT ARE YA DOING?" Iain demanded, violently pushing Niall back. It was too late. Jane was frozen in place. One of the plants she'd been attending withered, its life gone as Niall used it to cast the spell.

"Someone had to do something," Niall stated. To Euann, he ordered, "Her glove box. Get the potion. Her mouth is open. We can give it to her while she is petrified. Let's get this over with."

"Don't ya dare, Euann," Iain ordered.

"Sorry, Iain, ya know I like her too, but we have to know. That thing with the plants…" Euann moved to fetch the potion bottle from Jane's truck. "That wasn't just gardening. She's not a normal human."

"They're right," Rory said. "Aunt Margareta has good instincts. If your ma said we should worry, maybe we need to be sure."

"I was taking care of it," Iain said. "I said I'd handle it and I'll handle it. Jane is my responsibility. I just need a little more time to explain things to her."

"Ya had your chance last night and all day today. It's better to be sure," Niall said quietly, "before I have to erase her knowledge of us."

"No," Iain protested. "Ya can't erase me from

her life. I-I love her." He made a move to sweep Jane into his arms and carry her away from the gardens. The spell made her body as heavy as a boulder. "She accepts—"

Niall lifted his hand, and the yellow light shot forth again. Iain felt his body turning stone before he could protest. He was stuck mid-action trying to lift Jane. Rage filled him, and he wanted to strike out, but he couldn't. The spell was too strong, binding him from movement.

"If only your reasoning mattered more than what must be done." Niall gave him a pitying look, but Iain could only listen. "Don't worry. Once we know what she is, I'll be careful only to take those memories that I must. It will all be over before you wake."

Iain tried to respond but couldn't.

Niall crouched down and placed a hand on Iain's stiff shoulder. "Forgive me, brother, but there are too many lives at stake, and I will do what must be done. The clan must be protected."

Chapter Seventeen

Don't hurt Jane. Don't hurt Jane. Iain willed his family to hear his call from inside his petrified prison. He couldn't see beyond the fuzzy blur of his vision, couldn't feel his frozen limbs. But he could think. *Please, don't hurt my Jane.*

He had been petrified many times and knew his only option was to wait the spell out. Then, something strange happened. The haze around Iain's vision lifted.

He lay in a ditch with his older brother, Erik, in the country outside of town. A bonfire burned on the lawn across the road, casting orange shadows and outlining the unmistakable image of the tin star hanging in front of the driveway. It was Sheriff Johnson's home.

He remembered this place, these people, this

event. It was the night his power had been ripped from his body. Why had his mind brought him here, and with such clarity? This was a horrible night, one he wished he could forget. This was the night he should have died.

The sound of chanting filled the air, the words from some ancient Magyar dialect he couldn't translate. Erik's girlfriend, Lydia, kicked her feet as she was dragged by her bound wrists to be sacrificed.

But they'd saved Lydia. This was over. Iain didn't understand. He'd already lived this event. Lydia was marrying Erik. Charlotte was alive. The evil forces were stopped. Unless...

Niall.

Reliving this night could only be the work of magick. Was Niall in his head, pulling out memories? He always wondered what that would feel like. He'd met Jane after this event happened. Jane. He had to remember Jane. He couldn't let his brother erase her from his memory. His entire body wanted to run, away from this past, down the country road into town. He wanted to shift into bird form and fly away toward her. Jane. Home. Jane.

What had the potion revealed? What had they discovered about her that was so bad he couldn't know? What could possibly warrant their taking her from his mind? They never erased a family member's memories without consent…unless the circumstances were so dire, it was the only way to save the warlock's life. Iain wanted his memories, all of them. Centuries faded enough without them being manually erased.

Remember Jane. Remember Jane. Jane. Remember… remember…save Lydia. Save his brother's woman. Save his brother.

The current memory called him into it. Feelings of concern for his brother's girlfriend filled Iain. She was rare, a genetic anomaly of humankind that synced perfectly to one particular warlock. As an *inthrall*, Lydia could take Erik's power from him, use his magick, drain him, kill him or protect him. With the mere will to do so, she could absorb Erik's life. More to the point, she could be forced to take it from him. The *lidércs* who'd kidnaped her wanted to do just that—force Lydia to give them Erik's powers.

Iain worried for Erik. He worried for the clan should the *lidércs* be successful in their attempts to use Erik's *inthrall* against them. The *lidércs* were psychic vampires who controlled unsuspecting minds and lived as shadows. If they succeeded, they'd wreak havoc on the world. A thick log pole stuck in the lawn with a metal ring along the top. Iain hid with Erik across the dirt road in a ditch.

Townsfolk pulled a rope through the ring, hefting Lydia up the pole. When they finally had her several feet off the ground, they stopped and tied the rope on the star decoration near the side of the road. Her feet must have found hold on something because she stopped kicking and stood straighter. Erik tried to stand as if he would rescue the woman.

"Stop," Iain warned. "I know ya want to comfort her, but if you're not careful with your feelings, they'll detect us."

"I love her," Erik whispered.

"I love her?" Iain wasn't so much surprised by the revelation as he was the fact his brother admitted his feelings out loud. Hearing the words caused a tightness in his chest. A strange sensation pulled at his mind as if he should remember something, but nothing came to him. He couldn't imagine being in love. Warlocks lived for so many centuries that the odds of finding the one person he was meant to be with in all those years, in all those passing lifetimes, were immeasurable.

"What?" Erik demanded as if Iain had stepped on his territory.

"*Ya* said, 'I love her'." Iain didn't love Lydia. He cared for her, as much as anyone could care for someone they'd just met. She was important to Erik, which made her important to the rest of the clan. "Put your magick down and try to concentrate. No need to zap me. I think your lady friend is hot. I'm not going to ask her to have my babies."

Erik pointed a finger of warning but let the matter drop. "There, around the top of the fire. Do ya see it? A shadow."

"A *lidérc*." Iain nodded. Coldness crept into him as he watched the dancing shadow creature.

"We can't wait any longer," Erik insisted.

The possessed townsfolk continued to build an already blazing fire. The warlock brothers couldn't rush in with powerballs blazing and kill all the innocent humans being psychically held captive. However, Iain wasn't sure how much longer he could keep his brother calm. Erik was tormented to see the love of his life strung up on a pole. Unfortunately, that blind devotion was about to get his brother stripped of his magickal powers and killed. "Ya heard Da. We wait for them. We cannot fight the *lidércs* without the right magick. Lydia is alive. Take comfort in that."

"What are those people looking at on the far side of the fire?" Erik's nervous energy practically snapped off his skin.

"Ya rush in and they'll simply start the process early." Iain needed his brother to hear him. "Ya shouldn't even be here. Your connection to Lydia is the whole reason this is happening. You're too involved."

He didn't take Erik's answering growl of dismissal personally. "What are they looking at?"

"Someone's on the ground." Iain tried to be the voice of reason. He narrowed his eyes and focused on the prone body, using his shifter vision to zoom in. He saw Charlotte lying on the ground. Again, a strange feeling tried to invade him, but he shook it off. "Charlotte. She's not moving."

Lydia screamed in pain. Iain focused harder, trying to find signs of a pulse in Charlotte's neck. Suddenly, his eyes locked in their changed state and he couldn't look away from the unmoving body. He tried to physically jerk back, but old magick held him in its spell. Charlotte was a trap. The *lidércs* had used her as enchanted bait, waiting for any glimpse of MacGregor magick to come near her.

The pain started in his eyes and rolled through his body. The agony of it was unbearable, but Iain couldn't make it stop, couldn't scream as he desperately wanted to. He tried to warn his brother, but no sound came out. He held his chest, endeavoring to keep his power inside his body. It did no good. The entranced Charlotte forced the magick out of him like an empty chalice demanding to be filled. The human woman wasn't built to hold his powers. The transfer would surely kill her.

One of the *lidércs* circled overhead, waiting to drink Iain's magick from Charlotte. If that happened, the creatures would win, and they would be out to destroy his family. Helplessness mingled with the pain. Tears would have fallen, but the magick pulling out of his eyes wouldn't let them.

The entranced townsfolk turned toward the brothers' hiding place, chanting louder. Erik refused to run. Iain gasped for breath, unable to pull air deep into his withering lungs.

Slowly, the people formed a line along the far side of the road. He saw the shadowy impression of them before the bonfire light. The pain intensified as streams of his magick poured from his eyes and mouth toward Charlotte. Erik slapped his hand over Iain's face as if he could physically stop the process. When that didn't work, Erik tried to lift Iain's immobile body over his shoulder to carry him to safety. Seconds later, Iain found himself on the ground next to a collapsed Erik. He had the impression of being moved, but his eyes were blurry from their locked position.

This was death, coming in the hardest way possible. His magick was part of his very being. Without it, he was nothing more than a pile of bones and dust. This was it. He would never know the kind of love Erik fought for. Centuries passed before him, suddenly so short of a timespan. A tear managed to slide over his cheek, boiling hot enough to steam and burn his skin. Charlotte was taking everything. And in the moment before blackness set in, he heard the bagpipes of his youth calling to him. They beckoned his spirit to come home.

Home.

"Jane," his mind whispered, not knowing who she was, only that she meant home.

IAIN WOULDN'T HAVE MINDED the blackness surrounding him if he'd actually been passed out or asleep. Instead, he was incredibly aware of being stuck in a cold, dark place. He tried to use his magick, but Charlotte had left him drained. Aside from a residual pain that made him aware he still had at least bones for a body, he felt nothing. Was he still on the ground? Was this death? Limbo? Hell? A coma?

Fear filled him, but his circumstances gave him no way to retaliate against the darkness. He didn't eat, didn't sleep, didn't move. He thought he felt a brush against his arm, but he couldn't move his head to look, wasn't sure he even had a head anymore. Perhaps the pain radiating through what he thought was his body was really just his consciousness trying to hold on to normality. To anything.

"*Dè tha thu ag iarraidh?*" someone whispered. *What do you want?*

The airy words were so light they could have been an echo from his past. Iain tried to answer, but he had no mouth.

"*Dè tha thu ag iarraidh!*" the voice demanded.

Oh, how he wanted to answer it.

"I don't know what I want!" a woman screamed. He didn't know the voice, at least not that he remembered. He tried to focus, to hear where it came from within the darkness. Was someone inside his mind's tomb with him? Was he finally going to have company in the endlessness his existence had become?

The first sense to come back to him was smell. Faint traces of lilacs and purple Scottish heather surrounded him. Iain was sure he'd never smelled anything so wonderful in his life. Next came honey. He tasted it on his tongue. Then bagpipes in the distance. He knew that music. It filled his soul with memories of home. His family called to him. It had to be his family. They were trying to guide him back from oblivion.

No, wait. He felt something against his mouth. A kiss? The wet brush of a tongue? No magick his family would perform to call him home would involve such a sweet, intimate act. Like a mad rush, he felt his body return to him, and he was pulled from the dark hole of his mind.

The last sense to return to him was sight. Iain opened his eyes, desperate to make contact with the bearer of those gentle, saving lips. Windblown curls framed a beautiful face. Warmth replaced the cold. He felt love, so sure and intense that such an emotion could never be contained within one soul. Brown eyes flashed ever so briefly before disappearing altogether. Whoever she was, she was gone.

"Wait," Iain whispered desperately. She took her feelings of love with her. He was alive, awake, but the pain of losing something so beautifully perfect hurt worse than the oblivion he was pulled from. "Don't leave me."

Perhaps he was dead. His body was laid in a glass coffin. Trees surrounded him, their dark limbs like fingers across the sky. Iain tried to sit up so he could go look for her, but the effort weakened him. He fell back and then nothingness.

FEAR FILLED JANE, nearly choking the breath from her lungs. One moment she was weeding the MacGregor gardens, next Niall was threatening to make her drink a potion, and then she was thrust into what could only be a hallucination. Only this didn't feel like a hallucination. It felt more like déjà vu.

Jane remained rooted in place, like the wild overgrowth of the expansive gardens yearning to be saved. An aging woman yelled at her in Gaelic. She knew that wrinkled face. It was Iain's... It was... It was...

Memories began to slip into the moment.

"Why can I understand what you're saying?" Jane asked the stranger. "Who are you? How did I get here?"

The aging woman's finger dissipated into mist but did not disappear. Instead, the mist surrounded Jane's head. She swatted it away, but the action only caused the mist to swirl up her nose. The plants moved around her, coming to animated life. They stretched and grew, aging like the now-old woman before her, then transformed into a beautiful combination of lilac and purple Scottish heather. The heady scent of flowers and honey was so strong it burned her nostrils and caused her eyes to water. Bagpipes sounded in the distance, impossibly carried on a wind that did not stir.

The music called to her, offered to save her. The woman made a strange noise and collapsed on the ground. The instant the woman's body landed, Jane was freed. Instead of running home, she followed the retracting vines toward the bagpipes. She didn't know why, only that she was compelled to follow them. They led her deeper into the gardens. The smell of flowers followed her.

The vines began to shake and whither before falling to the ground. A patch of dead foliage formed a large circle around a glass coffin. Whatever had killed the weeds and bushes had started to infect the trees. Browned leaves clung to branches next to green ones.

A few dead vines crossed over the top as if hugging whoever lay inside. The encased figure was cast in shadow and did not move. The scene looked like something right out of a horrible fairy-tale, coffin placed on a stone altar in the middle of a lifeless patch of earth. Jane shivered as she stepped on the dried leaves and old vines. She felt something pulling at her legs, fatiguing her muscles.

The music grew sad as if begging someone to help. She found herself moving toward the coffin despite the tiredness in her limbs. For some reason, she had to see.

"Déjà vu," she whispered. The moment felt oddly familiar as if she'd walked this path many times.

Her hand shook as she reached to touch the glass case. She slid her fingers over the top, brushing aside crispy leaves. A man with dark hair was preserved perfectly inside. His skin did not look like a corpse's, but like that of a man sleeping, and yet his chest did not rise and fall with life. A rash darkened his cheek in the perfect trail of a tear.

Jane knocked on the glass, but he didn't open his eyes. The vibration of her interference caused the vines holding the lid to crack. The lid slid to the side without her pushing it. She held her breath, waiting to see what would happen.

Suddenly, something grabbed her wrist and jerked her hand down to his face. A healthy vine held her. She was forced to touch his warm skin. Her fingers tingled as if the man pulled life from her and in turn from the vine. Jane ran her thumb over his lips in a gentle caress. The gesture seemed to drag renewed color, and his lips parted. Breath finally whispered against her fingers.

"Get away from my son!"

Jane flinched and jerked her hand from the

man's face. As soon as the contact was severed, the vine on her wrist turned to dust, and her fingers stopped tingling. The frail old woman stood on the edge of the dead circle. She looked worse than before, her frame not much more than a skeleton in loose flesh.

"Get away from my son. I know what ya are, death's *reipseach*," the woman shouted. "*Thalla's cagainn bruis. Thalla's cagainn bruis!* I smell the death on ya. I will protect my house from your master. Ya cannot have my son. I have cast spells of protection. I have called to all the forces in the earth to help me bring him back. Ya cannot have him, death's *reipseach*. The forces are coming to save him. Go away. Ya cannot have my son."

Thalla's cagainn bruis?

Away and chew a brush?

What the hell kind of insult was that? And why could Jane understand that it was an insult? None of this made sense.

A ball of energy shot out of the woman's hand as she teetered on unsteady feet. The shaky aim was the only thing that kept the ball from hitting Jane's head. Jane yelled in fright and ran for the shelter of the nearby trees. Another shot fired and she felt a sizzle against her arm. Her legs were still weak from walking on the dead vines, and she tripped. Her head hit against the base of a stone statue of a woman surrounded by brush.

Time slipped, but somehow she managed to pull herself up and wander her way home. Her head ached, her legs burned, and when she pulled her tired body up the stairs, she collapsed near the couch, missing the soft cushions as she passed out on the hardwood floor.

Chapter Eighteen

"One word about my making a mistake and I'll hex ya, Angus MacGregor."

Jane stiffened at the threat and fought to open her eyes. Her hazy mind and heavy limbs felt as if she'd been drugged. No matter how much she wanted to move, she couldn't.

"What would I say, but ya look beautiful, my wife?" Angus answered.

Why was Margareta in her bedroom?

Why was Angus?

Wait. How was she? She was supposed to be working in the gardens.

No, they'd used magick on her and turned her to stone. They'd wanted to give her a potion. Niall wanted to do something to her.

A horrible taste coated her tongue, bitter and strange. Had they given her the potion?

Jane somehow managed to move her arm, dragging her elbow back to push her body up before her eyes even opened.

"She moves," Angus declared.

"Quiet," Margareta scolded. "Don't hover over the girl."

Jane opened her eyes to find Angus's face near hers. She gasped and fell back. Her head bounced lightly on the soft mattress.

"Wha-ah-eesh," she said. The words sounded strange, even though her brain tried to say, *What is happening?*

"Good morning, dear," Margareta pushed her husband out of the way. "Ya are coming out of the spell. Give it a moment. Your thoughts will align. The memories of the past will fill in."

Jane narrowed her eyes in concern. It was about all the movement she could manage. Though her body didn't obey her mind, that didn't mean her mind wasn't sharp. Iain's mother looked sixty years younger than the woman she'd seen being pushed in the wheelchair...than the aging woman in the gardens throwing electric magick balls at her.

Coffin.

Iain.

"Iain," she mumbled, again trying to stir. She remembered Iain trapped in the gardens. Hallucination? Real? It felt real. Iain's mother was indicating it was real.

"Sleeping," Margareta said.

Jane blinked, confused. She had a hard time concentrating.

Margareta reached to touch her cheek, and Jane's widening eyes followed the woman's hand. Iain's mother had tried to kill her. She'd found Iain asleep in the forest, and all she'd wanted to do was help, but Margareta had tried to set her on fire with a magick ball. Fear filled her as a tear slipped from her eyes. Margareta brushed the moisture away. Leaning over, she smiled. "Ya woke up too quickly. Ya should be asleep as well. It will make the transition out of the potion's spell easier."

Jane didn't trust that smile. She tried to shake her head, the only gesture she could make to stop whatever Margareta planned. The woman lifted her other hand holding a small bottle, dripping translucent orange liquid between Jane's eyes. She closed her lids, trying to keep the potion out of her eyes. It didn't work. Liquid pooled outside her lids. Sleep came swiftly.

IAIN SHOT UP IN BED, instantly levitating above his mattress. Power snapped through him, and for a long moment, he merely hovered, arms reaching wide, legs dangling. His mind swam with thoughts, incoherent and broken—Charlotte near a bonfire taking the life out of him, death, pain, the end, a pair of beautiful eyes, coffin glass distorting the sky, the tingle of magick entering his mouth to give him life, the beginning.

Those eyes. Jane.

Remember Jane.

After the *lidércs* had nearly killed him, he'd been kept in a preservation coffin. Jane had saved his life. He'd needed her and she'd come. Why hadn't he remembered? Why didn't she tell him? Did she even remember? It must have been some powerful magick if they'd forgotten about it.

Jane.

Instinct took over. Iain cried out as his muscles became so stiff his bones snapped. Though his transformation was based in magick, it didn't stop the contracting of his body from hurting. His heart beat faster. As he became smaller, feathers were pushed out of his skin like tiny needles. His feet hardened and cracked apart, forming large talons.

There was a wild energy to being in bird form as if his warlock magick was amplified within the smaller size. He flapped his wings, instinctually trying to find freedom. At first he went to the window, but it was closed. His wings beat against the glass.

Conscious thought came in a focused stream.

Remember Jane. Find Jane.

Jane.

In that moment, his life depended on that one thought. Jane. He had to find her. He had to stop whatever his family wanted to do to her. He had to protect her from Sean. He had to stop Niall from taking her memories. He had to save her from all the dangers of the world.

Jane.

When it became apparent he wasn't flying through glass, he changed directions and flew along the ceiling, trying to find a way outside. He circled the room and finally landed on the end of his bed. There was no way out, and yet he remained desperate to find one. He tilted his head and listened, perched and tense. Footsteps.

"Iain? That ya moving around?" Raibeart opened the bedroom door and poked his head in.

Iain took the opportunity and dove toward his uncle's face. Raibeart screamed and ducked. Iain turned, bumping into the heavy door on his way through before sweeping through the home.

"Eagle in flight! Eagle in flight!" Raibeart yelled after him. "Man the windows, lads!"

Iain went toward a window. A shot of magick passed him, slamming the glass down. He turned, following the subtle shift of air flow for another opening. Euann and Rory were running around the bottom level, manually pulling windows closed and latching them.

"The fireplace," Rory said. "Stop him!"

"Iain, over here," Euann yelled to get his bird brother's attention. He flapped his arms widely, trying to distract while Rory magickally produced bricks to block the fireplace chimney.

Iain squawked in frustration. Upstairs, he heard doors slamming shut as they sought to contain him.

"Stun him, lads," Raibeart ordered.

"What's going on out here?" Angus appeared along the top rail.

"Bird boy's loose," Euann answered, "and I'm trying to make fried chicken."

Iain dodged Euann and Rory's attempts to stun him. Magick blasted along the ceiling and walls, making a mess.

"Don't hurt your brother," Angus demanded.

"We're just trying to stop him," Rory said.

"We can't let him get out," Euann said.

"Someone has been out shooting in the woods. Ruined all my cameras."

"Poachers?" Angus asked in fear. He hurried to the top of the stairs. He lifted his unprotected arm as if ready to catch a falcon. "Iain, come here, my boy."

"Wrong bird form," Raibeart said. "The eagle never listens. Besides, he'll tear your arm off if he lands there."

"Iain," Angus demanded more insistently, still holding out his arm. "Ya can't leave. It's not safe."

"Find your nest or you'll be a ten-piece chicken basket," Raibeart said.

"Not helping," Angus answered.

Iain watched all of this but didn't really process it. He needed to find Jane. None of these things were Jane.

With only one option of escape left, he built up speed, tucked his head and dove into a glass pane. He prepared for impact, knowing it was going to hurt.

"Nay!" Angus yelled. Seconds before he would have crashed through, the window disappeared and he was free. The air felt wonderful against his wings, and for a moment, he soared high above the mansion on the hill, enjoying the freedom. It was a short-lived celebration as Jane once again took the forefront of his thoughts. The longer he stayed shifted, the harder it would be to remain focused. Soon the wild would take over.

Find Jane. Remember Jane.

Iain didn't know exactly where he should look, but he turned toward the nursery. He focused his eyes and looked for her like a hunter seeking his prey.

Find Jane.

Protect Jane.

Chapter Nineteen

Jane woke up swinging. Her fist contacted flesh as she scrambled to get out of the bed. A light gasp of surprise met the strike. Thankfully, movement had returned to her limbs, and she used every ounce of energy to escape whatever fate awaited her. Her legs tangled in bedding, and she kicked. Somehow, her wild exodus from the bed landed her on the floor. She stood, arms raised, ready to charge anyone who stood in her way.

Margareta held her cheek. Jane couldn't help the small feeling of pleasure at seeing who she'd struck. Then, taking in the older face, she felt instantly guilty.

"I'm sorry. I didn't mean to hit you, but, you…" Jane edged for the door. Margareta didn't try to stop her. "I'm leaving. I don't know what you were doing to me, but—"

"Ya sound better," Margareta answered calmly. She dropped her hand, and her cheekbone was bright red beneath one eye. "And you're no longer drooling. That's a good sign."

"I'm leaving." Jane held up one hand and reached for the door with the other. "Don't try to stop me. And I'm sorry about your eye, but Iain needs me. He's in the... He's in the coffin. He's in the..."

"I probably deserve worse after how I treated ya," the woman answered.

"Well, I think you deserve... Wait, what?" Jane frowned, hand on the knob but not pulling it open.

"If ya tell anyone I apologized, I'll deny it. I am the matriarch of this clan after all, but I regret how I acted. In my defense, I didn't remember ya saved my son's life, and ya can hardly fault a woman for trying to protect her family."

"Wait, what?" Jane tilted her head in confusion. "But the coffin. It was Iain. The coffin. He needs me. Can't you hear the bagpipes calling me to come? I have to go to him."

"Breathe, dear, your thoughts will align."

"What did you do to Iain? Why is he in the coffin?" Jane looked at the window. It was bright daylight. Fear and confusion swam inside her. Only one fact remained prominent and clear, she needed to save Iain. "Is he...coffin?"

She couldn't say *dead*.

"He's fine, thanks to ya. Iain and Erik were in fight trying to save Lydia and Charlotte. Iain was severely injured. I used all my powers to save my son from death, but it wasn't enough, so I preserved him," Margareta said. She didn't move or show signs of aggression. She kept her hands down at her sides. "After he was attacked, I worked an enchantment spell, placed him in a preservation coffin and put him in the gardens to help his magick rejuvenate. I then used every spell I know to help him. A mother will kill herself to save her child. But ya saved him. I don't know how ya did it, but ya came to the gardens and gave him life."

"So they're all right? Everyone's fine?"

"Breathe, Jane. It only feels like it just happened because ya re-experienced the events. From what I can gather, this happened before ya officially met my son, before Erik proposed. So, yes, everyone is—"

"Charlotte," Jane interrupted.

"Is recovering. Slowly." Margareta sighed. "We are doing what we can to help her. The townsfolk who were there think they were dosed with magic mushrooms in a potluck casserole."

Jane remembered talking to Alana about that very event. "I don't understand."

"How did ya find Iain in the forest?"

"I followed the bagpipes. It was an impulse I couldn't fight." Jane frowned, starting to remember the events more clearly. "What happened to him? Why was he in there? Why am I only now just remembering doing this?"

"Psychic vampires poisoned Charlotte in hopes of using her as a vessel to drain Iain's magick out of him so they could make themselves corporeal. It almost worked. We stopped the threat, but Iain nearly died. Some would argue that he did die and was stuck in limbo."

"And you think Charlotte is recovering? I saw her the other night. She didn't look well."

"She's being looked after. Ya mustn't mention this to her. She's very fragile. We had to take the memory of the event from her. The knowledge of what happened was too hard for her to live with. Lydia and Erik have her under their care."

"Why am I only now remembering my part in this?"

"The magick I used was strong. It's possible healing him took a lot out of ya, just as summoning help took a lot out of me." Margareta made a move as if she would touch her. "We both didn't remember what happened until Niall gave ya the potion and we could see the events for what they were. Since Iain was touching ya when ya drank it, there were a few unexpected side effects. Iain relived his memories of the events, as well."

Jane lifted a finger in warning as she tried to sort her thoughts. "So the aging?"

"As I said, a mother will kill herself to save a child. Preserving Iain in the coffin took a lot out of me. It's a good thing too, if I'd been at full strength, I might have stopped ya from saving him."

"The sound of bagpipes pied pipered me to the gardens. I found Iain and somehow my touch saved him? You attacked me." Jane frowned. The memories were clearer with each second, but the truth of it was so surreal. "Why did you try to kill me if I was there to help?"

"Spells are not always an exact science, more of an art or an educated guess. The results can be surprising. The bagpipes called you to help him. It was destiny that ya two should meet. But when I sensed what ya are, I thought ya had come to claim his soul."

"Sensed what I am?" Jane shook her head. "I don't understand. Aside from my ability to grow plants, I'm not special. I'm not magickal."

"The death in ya," Margareta said. "Cait read your hand. We know your life line has been interrupted many times."

"Is that why everyone keeps thinking I'm something I'm not? That's because I'm dying," Jane said. "I'm told many people who walk close to death all the time often see through the veil to the other side. I see ghosts because I'm dying, and they sometimes like to follow me once they find out I can communicate with them. If you sense anything, it's that. I'm not anything special."

Margareta scowled. "How can ya say such? Ya saved my son's life. Ya saved mine because I would have surely died trying to help him. The MacGregors owe ya—"

Jane's hand on the door knob was thrust to the side as the door swung open. Angus glanced at her in surprise before saying to his wife in a worried tone, "Iain's out."

"What's wrong?" Jane demanded.

"Out?" Margareta repeated. "Out-out?"

Angus nodded adamantly. "He's over the forest. Euann said there have been poachers."

"Ah, about that," Rory said behind his uncle. He poked his head in the door. "Hey, Jane." Jane didn't answer as she silently willed them to tell her what was wrong with Iain. "That was me. I used Euann's cameras as target practice. I'm sure Iain will be fine. Once he calms down, he'll shift back, and we'll go pick him up."

"Ya shot my cameras?" Euann demanded in anger from the hallway.

"Well, ya shouldn't have sent those pictures of me examining my bleeding ass to the family," Rory answered. "A man's got a right to privacy in his own woods."

"Enough." Angus pushed Rory behind him to get him out of the room. "Argue about the family's Christmas card photos later."

"Will someone please tell me what is wrong with Iain?" Jane insisted.

"He's had a small incident. It's nothing to be overly worried about, but he's locked in an altered form for the moment. The potion we used to discover your intentions had a strange side effect and hit him too. The two of ya were petrified at the same time, and he was touching ya. When he came out of it, his hold over his inner bird slipped, and he transformed into an eagle," Angus said.

"And now he's outside, flying around, stuck as a bird?" Jane clarified.

Angus nodded, looking as if he half-expected Jane to have a panic attack. What was it with these MacGregors acting like humans couldn't handle a little bit of magick and supernatural?

"Why are we standing here?" Jane said,

moving to slip past Angus. "Let's go get him back."

JANE WASN'T SURE HOW, but she found herself standing outside her nursery, gazing up at the trees. A large eagle stared down at her. She'd seen those shifted eyes before.

"Iain?" she asked. His head turned as if he knew her.

"Easy, lassie," Angus whispered, edging up behind her. "He will tear ya apart with his talons. He's not the Iain ya know right now." Angus took her by her arm and tried to pull her away with him.

At the sight of his father, Iain flapped his long wings and dove toward them. Jane stumbled. Angus made a small sound of surprise. When Jane glanced back, she saw Angus holding his bloody forearm.

Iain perched on a lower branch, eyeing his father as if daring him to touch Jane again.

"He's protective of ya," Angus observed.

"I have this," Jane said, keeping her tone even. "Give us space."

"I don't like leaving ya to handle my son. Let

me petrify him in flight and the boys can catch him when he falls," Angus said.

"Then what? You have a frozen bird for a son?" Jane shook her head.

"We'll get him locked in a cage until we can talk him out of it. He hasn't been gone long. It should only take a few weeks to get him to come out of it." Angus gestured that she should back away.

"Bird Iain seems to like me," Jane said. "Let me see if I can talk him down."

"I don't like it." Angus hesitated, but then she heard him back away to the other side of the greenhouse. "Lydia was able to calm Erik's beast; perhaps ya can help Iain. Careful. We'll be right behind this building. If he makes one false move, we'll stun him."

When she was alone with the eagle, Jane lifted her hand. "Iain? What are you doing? Everyone is worried about you. Please, come down from there."

Iain flapped his wings several times before leaving his perch to land on the ground in front of her. Jane kneeled. For a bird, he was large. For an Iain, he was tiny. She tried to touch him.

"Lassie?" Angus called.

Iain snapped at her fingers. She snatched her hand back.

"Hey, who are you snapping at?" Jane scolded. Then louder, she said, "Give me a moment."

Iain rocked back and forth as he walked toward her, head slightly down. He stopped near her hand. She hesitantly touched along his back feathers.

"All right, transform back now," she said. He merely looked at her. She dropped her hand. "I'm serious, Iain. Put your man parts on. Grow arms." She held her hands to the side and shook her fingers. Nothing. Jane dropped her hands and sighed. Sarcastically, she mumbled, "Dammit, Iain, as if seeing ghosts isn't strange enough. As if dating a warlock isn't weird. As if being told I had the starring role as Prince Charming to awaken your Sleeping Beauty ass from a coffin—really, a coffin? But now I also get a bird boyfriend? Are you really going to make me the crazy bird lady who is having a romance with her pet eagle?"

Iain made a strange bird noise.

"You all make me crazy, Iain MacGregor. Your mother magickally called me to save you, I hear bagpipes all the time and hallucinate Scottish moors. I stole energy from plants to get you out of a coffin your mother put you in all because she cast a spell that apparently knew we were each other's destiny. I'm talking to a bird, who is a man that I've slept with... I don't even want to finish that line of thought. This is insanity. The whole lot of you are insane, and you are making me insane." She crossed her arms over her chest. "I'm going to need you to give me one good reason as to why I shouldn't jump in my truck and keep driving."

Iain began to shake and emitted a burning smell. Jane wrinkled her nose and tried not to breathe too deeply as she backed away. His skin stretched, pushed out from within. She flinched at how painful it looked. The bird body extended to one side and then contracted before reaching in the other direction. Suddenly, the creature exploded. Jane screamed and fell back.

"Jane, we're coming, lassie," Angus yelled. She heard feet running. Iain emerged, growing from within the feathered husk.

"It's all right," she answered, lifting her hand to stop them from charging in. Iain gasped for breath and stopped shaking.

A power surge shot over her. It hit her hand, instantly stiffening her fingers and weighing them down. It dropped to her lap. The magick hit Iain, freezing him into statue form. He kneeled naked before her, brown eyes with flecked with green stuck in her direction. There was something very erotic about the Iain statue before her, sculpted male perfection, but she didn't want to be caught staring at his naked form as his family surrounded her.

"Get the wheelbarrow," Angus ordered. "Let's get him home before anyone sees."

"I have the perfect place for him," Euann said. "Right in the garden fountain. We need a statue there."

"Euann," Angus chided. "Ya will put him in his room."

Jane's arm began to ache and then her chest as if her blood couldn't flow. "Ah, help?" She gasped, trying to rub the frozen digits.

"Ach, sorry, Jane, this won't last long," Euann said. He lifted his hand. Before she could protest, he was freezing the rest of her. "We'll make sure you're locked safely inside your home before we go."

Chapter Twenty

"Sorry about your tomatoes," Jane read the sticky note that had been stuck to her forehead when she unthawed from the petrifying spell. "Call if you need assistance."

Jane looked up from the note to her dead tomato plants. When the MacGregors had cast the petrifying spell, they'd killed off seventy percent of her tomatoes. The loss was heartbreaking, but she could hardly fault them for trying to help Iain. Still, what was she going to do now? Tomatoes were her best sellers. She couldn't grow new ones overnight. Or could she? Looking at her hands, she thought about weeding the MacGregor garden and how the men had reacted to the plant's rejuvenation.

"Why are you avoiding me?"

Jane jerked in surprise. It took her a moment to process who'd spoken. Sean stood several yards away with his arms crossed over his chest. Guilt instantly assaulted her as she looked at his face. She'd forgotten all about him. "Oh, no, dinner. I'm sorry. Something important came up." She gestured at her garden. "I—"

"I can take a hint, Jane. I know you're not happy to see me. I don't know what I did, what we did." Sean gave a dramatic pause and looked toward the sky. "Mother was inconsolable when you didn't come back to see her."

"I'm sorry about Dana. I know it isn't easy—"

"I promised her I would find you and try to…" He shook his head and then looked toward the ground. "But you won't even have dinner with me. You won't spend any time with me. All I want to do is honor our mother's memory, and you won't let me. Tell me what I need to do."

"Sean, please." Jane took a deep breath. There was something about his expression, a sadness and desperation, that made her feel sorry for him. She couldn't do anything about her dead garden, and if she stayed where she was staring at it, then she'd only stress herself out, so she said, "Let me change my clothes. We'll go right now. Lunch. We'll talk about whatever you want."

Sean nodded and quickly smiled. "Splendid, Jane. I'll wait for you."

But he didn't wait, not really. He followed her into her building and up to her apartment as if he expected her to try to escape out a window. Jane changed her clothes with an eye on her bedroom doorknob to make sure he didn't open it. He was waiting for her in the hall when she finished.

"Ready?" he asked, lifting his hand to indicate she should move past him and lead the way.

Jane did her best to smile. What was one dinner? There was no reason to put it off any longer if that meant Sean would finally be on his way and leave her town once and for all.

"YA SHOULD HAVE BROUGHT HER HERE," Iain said, pulling on a clean shirt. "Ya should not have left her frozen and alone."

"It was hard enough carting one of ya to the mansion," Euann defended. He lounged on Iain's bed, absently gesturing his fingers, so tiny dots of magick sprinkled over his face. "We put her in her home and I left her a note. Ya worry too much."

"Ya should not have frozen her," Iain continued.

"We were aiming for our birdbrain brother,"

Euann defended, his voice contradicting the easy nature of his position on the bed. "Her arm was in the way. It was easier to freeze the rest of her than to make her suffer. Besides, how were we to know she could talk ya into changing back?"

"Lydia did it for Erik," Iain said.

"Are ya saying Jane is your *fíorghrá*?" Euann sat up on the bed. "Have ya told Ma? After what we hear Jane did for ya, I'm sure she'll want to plan another wedding. Ma told us how she saved ya with her garden magick. Only, there is one thing we're still not clear on. What is Jane? She can't just be human."

"She said her birth mother took off when she was very young. Her mother's heritage is unknown."

Euann chuckled. "What if she really is half *shellycoat*? I've seen pictures of them. She might not age too well."

"I'm going to see Jane," Iain said by way of an answer. "Do not follow me."

"YOU WORK TOO MUCH. You need help." Sean lifted his fork and took a tiny bite of chicken fried rice like the Chinese all-you-can-eat buffet was the same as snooty five-star cuisine. Jane bit into an egg roll to keep from having to answer. "Someone with business sense. I'd be willing to take over for you and help take your business to the next level."

Jane choked and began to cough. She reached for her water glass.

He handed her a paper napkin and kept talking. "I think we'd make great partners. You do the manual labor. I can make sure the store is stocked of supplies. You have an entire storefront you are not utilizing properly."

"You..." She took a drink of water. "You want to be a landscaper?"

"Business is business," he said. "You said yourself that your mother is out of the picture. So your only relative, I'm already legally able to inherit it from you. Being partners will make that easier. Not to be insensitive, but you've been sick for a long time. Wouldn't you like to know your business is in good hands? My hands? I can have my lawyer draw up partnership paperwork if you like?"

"I'm not looking for a partner." Jane envisioned him giving all her vegetables to Mrs. Callister free of charge. She needed to change the subject quickly. "Um, you said you wanted to talk about your mother?"

"Oh, ah, yes." He nodded and set down his fork. "You know, Mother loved you."

Jane didn't know that, but she didn't see a reason to point it out.

"She took you in as if you were her own after your mother abandoned you. Not many women would be as selfless as my mother was. And I never threw a fit about how she treated you. I accepted you as my sister." There was a slight accusation to his tone.

Jane took another big bite and told herself to keep chewing so she wouldn't be tempted to answer him. That's not exactly how she recalled their childhood, but whatever. Arguing the finer points of blended families was not how she wanted to spend her day. If she stayed quiet, maybe he'd get to a point. Probably not.

"She deserved better than to die the way she did because of..." Sean waved his hand and refused to finish.

Jane forced herself to swallow the giant mouthful and gave a small cough. "Because of?"

Sean's brow furrowed, and Jane could envision the cogs in his brain working. "I don't remember what I was going to say."

She didn't believe him.

"You might not have realized it, but Mother wasn't perfect. She wasn't all that good with finances. The reason I wanted to speak to you is I found some money I think you should have. It was in an account in your father's name. It was left to my mother, but I think she'd want you to have it."

"I thought all that money was gone," Jane said.

"She wasn't hiding it on purpose," Sean defended.

"I didn't mean to imply—"

"It's not like you always make the best decisions," Sean said. "Take that man you're seeing. What's his name? Igor?"

"Iain," Jane corrected in irritation.

"You can do much better. I'm sure it hasn't been easy, but Iain? Jane, really." Sean waved his fork in dismissal. "Mother would have wanted you to have the money. I have the paperwork in my hotel room. You'll come with me after and—"

"Sean, stop." Jane put down her fork and slid her plate to the side. "What is this? You want to see me because I'm family? Then you want to run my business and my love life? Now you suddenly have money from my father? Why do I have the feeling you're not telling me something important?"

"I'm not hiding anything." He refused to look her in the eye.

"I didn't say you were hiding something," Jane clarified. Though, now that he mentioned it…

"So you really don't know anything about your birth mother?"

"Why do you keep asking about her?" Jane didn't want to talk about her birth mother. She barely even thought about the woman anymore… well, not until recently when Sean kept bringing the subject of mothers up.

"Just making conversation."

"Make a different conversation," Jane quipped. She felt herself losing her temper and took a deep breath.

"You're overwhelmed," he stated. "I understand. It's not easy for you being all alone." Sean reached forward and grabbed her hand. "It's all right. I'm here now. You don't have to act so tough."

"You've already talked to a lawyer about the partnership, haven't you?" Jane wondered if Sean ever really heard her when she spoke. "The papers are in your hotel room, aren't they? That's why you really want me to go."

"I knew you'd see reason," he answered with a smile. "You'll feel better once you sign them and take some of the burden off your shoulders."

Realizing it was pointless to argue with him, she pulled the plate back in front of her if only to block his attempts at handholding and tried to finish her meal. He spoke. She nodded. He talked some more. She nodded some more and pretended to listen.

When the waitress arrived with the check, Sean stood. "You'll want to come with me back to the hotel for those papers. I'll get the car."

He left without offering to help pay for the check. Jane sighed and grabbed her purse. It's not like the car was valet parked. It was two stalls from the front door.

Jane had no intention of going to Sean's hotel room. He'd probably find a way to stick her with the bill for his stay. She wasn't sure what her step-brother expected to gain from this family outing besides a way to muscle his way into her business. If she signed him on as a partner, he'd probably drain her bank account and sell off everything the second she turned her back on him.

The MacGregors might have their issues, but they were what a family should be. She'd tried with Sean. It was all she could do. They'd had their dinner and now that it was over, she could go to the MacGregor estate and check on Iain, and Sean could get in his shiny car and drive away into the sunset where she would never see him again.

Chapter Twenty-One

Thump.

Thump.

Thump.

Jane moaned, as her head bounced against the ground.

Thump.

Thump.

At first, it was only the sensation of movement. Then the pain set in. Her arms dragged over her head as she was pulled by her feet. Her head bumped against the uneven forest path.

"Ow." Jane tried to stop moving. Her fists clenched and unclenched as she attempted to grab on to passing nature. She weakly lifted her head. Sean had her by her ankles. The last thing she remembered was telling him she wasn't getting into his car and then starting the walk back home. "Sean? What are you doing?"

"Here she is!" Sean called up into the trees. He dropped her legs. "I brought her just like you wanted."

Jane dug her heels into the ground and pushed back to get away from him. When she tried to stand, she swayed and fell on her side. Sean had drugged her. Her neck ached. Her back burned as if scraped raw. She wobbled as she tried to get on her hands and knees.

"I promised I'd bring her to you," Sean yelled. He grabbed her foot and jerked her toward him when she tried to crawl away. "Where are you?"

Jane kicked, but the gesture lacked force. "Let me go."

"Here she is, as promised. Come feed!" Sean searched the tops of the trees before going to peer into the dark forest. "Mother? Mother, can you hear me?"

"Mother?" Jane pushed to her feet. Why was Sean calling for his dead mother? "Sean, what are you doing? Dana is dead. You told me so yourself."

"Shut up!" He slashed his hand toward Jane. "This is your fault. You left me no choice. You ran away, and it couldn't find you."

"It?" Jane held the back of her aching head.

A frightening cackle echoed down from the trees. Jane searched the limbs, finding a white blur of movement jumping from branch to branch. The figure stopped out of reach, and the throat-popping noise grew louder from that direction. The being jumped again, pausing long enough for Jane to make out wrinkled skin and thin arms.

The blur shot forward to stand a few feet away from her. Jane gave a short scream of surprise to see the old woman. Her heart pounded, and she felt her throat tightening. Milky brown eyes were tinged with red. Long white hair flowed around her bony face. The tattered, dirt-stained white robe had seen better days. Long nails curved almost like claws as the creature reached toward Jane. There was something very familiar about the woman-creature.

"Dana? Is that you?" Jane whispered, unable to look away. "What is she? What happened to her?"

"That hideous thing is not *my* mother. It killed my mother because you ran. It couldn't find you, so it came after us." Sean gripped Jane's arm and tried to force her toward the tree creature. "Here she is, banshee. I kept my promise. Where is my mother? You promised if I found Jane for you, you'd give my mother back to me."

"Washerwoman," Jane said, realizing where

she'd seen the woman. "By the water. You're a banshee, a *bean nighe*. You're why the MacGregors have been sensing death around me. You're a death omen."

"Little Jane," the *bean nighe* said, her words much clearer than would be expected from such a physical presence.

"My mother," Sean demanded. "A deal is a deal. I poured that liquid on Jane and brought her to you just like you told me to."

"Little Jane, so long." The *bean nighe* ignored Sean.

"I saw you by the water not that long ago," Jane answered.

"I do not see when I work, only the clothes that must be cleaned." The *bean nighe* stared, appearing enamored with Jane's face. She moved closer, completely docile as if she wished to calm a flighty creature—and Jane was the creature.

"Banshee, your promise. My mother!" Sean yelled for attention.

The docile *bean nighe* instantly changed, opening her mouth to screech in anger toward Sean. The wind around her stirred, blowing leaves from the forest floor straight into the air. When the creature stopped, the leaves fluttered all around them and a worn burlap sack lay at Sean's feet.

"What's this? We had a deal." Sean leaned down and untied the old string around the top of the bag. He pinched the bottom corners and turned the sack over to empty the contents. A pile of human bones fell at his feet. He inhaled sharply and threw the sack aside as he jumped back.

"Our deal is met," the *bean nighe* stated. "Be gone."

"What?" Sean made a growling noise of frustration. "You promised to return my mother to me. I saw you take her soul. Give it back. You said you'd…" As if the gruesome realization dawned on him, he looked at the bones. "No. No, you said…you promised. Bring her back. You said you'd give her to me. You said if I found Jane, you'd give my mother back to me. You said. You said. You…" Sean gathered up the bones that had scared him moments before. He hugged them to his chest as he began to cry. "Mother?"

"What do you want from me?" Jane asked. She couldn't deal with Sean's crazy right now.

"Don't you remember me, little Jane?" the *bean nighe* asked.

Jane shook her head in denial. The creature walked with labored steps, as if traveling by ground was much more difficult than flying through trees. Jane worked her feet against the forest floor to keep distance between them. Her body ached with each movement as she scurried back.

"I'm so tired, little Jane," the *bean nighe* said. The red in her eyes became more pronounced.

"Mother," Sean cried. "No. No…"

"Sean," Jane tried to sound stern to get his attention. "We have to go now."

"You still reek of warlock," the *bean nighe* continued. "But their magick is not as strong on you."

"Sean, move," Jane ordered.

"I looked for so long," the banshee said. "I can wait no longer."

"It's my time, isn't it?" Jane whispered. "I'm dying. That's why you're here."

"I can already feel the ghosts calling to me. I can't go back, Jane." The *bean nighe* lifted both hands as if she expected Jane to come to her.

Though every part of her wanted to live, Jane found herself standing and moving toward the creature. Her body reacted as if the muscle memories embedded in her limbs remembered what to do. The smell of musty death emitted from the *bean nighe*, the perfume of grave dust and moldy clothes. Bony hands reached for Jane's face.

"Do you remember me now?" The *bean nighe* touched Jane's cheeks.

Jane gasped at the contact. Sorrow filled her,

pouring out of her heart to cause her entire body to ache physically. She did remember this. The story of her childhood was in those red-brimmed eyes and chapped mouth. Part of her soul stirred within the milky gaze peering back into her. The *bean nighe's* lips parted, revealing the rotted fangs of her teeth. Even as she knew what was to come, Jane couldn't resist it. This was her fate. She'd known it as a little girl staring into the abyss, as a teenager weakened and resigned and tired of hospitals, and now as a woman who had everything to live for but understood that willpower alone could not create life in death. A small smile formed on the *bean nighe's* mouth the second realization dawned on Jane's face. "Hello, my little Jane."

"Hello, Mom," Jane answered. With her birth mother's touch came clarity. Her mom hadn't left her. Her mom was a *bean nighe*. The sorrow grew, becoming the unbearable depression that haunted her in the darkest of moments. Jane suddenly remembered why she was dying.

"It's time you take my place so that I can finally rest." The creature's expression softened, but Jane did not mistake tenderness for a mother's love. "You were not supposed to live very long in this human form."

Jane didn't need to ask if it would hurt. She

knew her answer. The agonizing pull of life leaving her body would burn like the pits of hell were exploding inside her. Forgetfulness was the only real gift her mother had given her, the blank slate that took these horrific moments from her until the next touch, the next feeding. A mother's touch was supposed to bring comfort. Her mother only brought sickness.

The *bean nighe's* mouth opened wide. Jane braced herself for what was to come. The tingling started in her toes and fingers, pulling up through her limbs, burning as the blood stopped flowing in her veins. Tears streamed down her cheeks. She'd been prepared for death, living on the hope of an afterlife haunting the forest and greenhouse she'd come to love. But her fate was much worse. She was to become the thing that killed her. She was to take her mom's place as a *bean nighe*.

The loud squawk of a bird shook Jane from her trance. *Iain.*

The *bean nighe's* body jerked forward without warning. Her grip slipped and she released Jane. The memories of Jane's past slipped and began to fade.

Sean swung a stick at the creature's back. "I want what you promised!"

The *bean nighe* screeched and turned her attention to the attacker. She flew forward, blurring toward the man only to reappear in front of him. She pulled his life force from him with a harsh inhale. Severe age marred Sean's handsome face.

"No, leave him!" Jane yelled. She surged forward. She grabbed the creature's shoulders from behind. The rush of memory filled her once more at the contact. "Mom, let him go. You can't feed on living humans. Let him go."

Iain swooped in from the trees, talons drawn to slice the creature's arms. The *bean nighe* dropped Sean and turned her attention toward Iain.

"No!" Jane screamed as her mother tried to blur off into the trees. She held on tightly, flying with her. Jane lifted off the ground before their combined weight pulled the *bean nighe* back down. She reached for a sucker tree and grabbed hold with one hand while gripping the *bean nighe* with the other. In her desperation to stop the attack, she felt herself transferring life from the *bean nighe* to the sucker. Despite what she was, the *bean nighe* was still her mother, and that genetic connection fueled her sorrow. "Mom, I'm sorry, but you have to stop."

The creature screeched. Even as she did it, regret filled Jane. She felt the hollowness of souls passing through her. The tree truck thickened and outgrew her fisted hold.

This is what the *bean nighe* wanted—her own

death. She wanted Jane to replace her, to end her suffering. The screeching stopped. Milky eyes stared at her. Her mom smiled. There was relief in the expression, a peace that had never been there.

"Thank you." Her mom's words whispered through Jane's mind. Then the creature let go, blowing through Jane, filling her with the pain of death before transferring life into the tree.

All around Jane, the forest bloomed. Plants covered the forest floor in vibrant greens and whites, reaching into the shadowed corners. The sucker tree had become a forest giant with long sweeping branches that reached over her head.

Iain landed on the ground before her. His feet touched the new undergrowth and it triggered a transformation back into his human form. He kneeled before her naked. Blood marred his fingertips where he'd scratched the *bean nighe*.

"Jane?" he whispered. "What happened?"

"She's gone." Jane shook her head in an effort to clear it.

"Ya called her your ma."

"She's my birth mother. She came to me when I was younger. She's the reason I've been so ill. I remembered everything when she touched me. This is what she wanted. Well, not exactly this. She wanted me to take her place so that she could be free of her curse. I don't think this is exactly how she foresaw that happening." Jane looked up the giant tree. She felt her mom's energy flowing inside the bark underneath her hand.

Jane pulled her hand from the tree she'd grown. She frowned, feeling as if her memory was slipping into her subconscious as she stopped touching the back. "She went through me. She gave me...something." She touched the tree again, and her memories cleared once more. "She wanted me to take her place, but I didn't. Something else happened. I'm her daughter, so she could feed off me, but she was not supposed to feed off humans. So, when she fed off Sean, something weakened inside of her, and I was able to absorb her and put her into this tree instead of taking her curse into my body."

"Ya are half *bean nighe*. That has to explain your ability to transfer energy. Legend has it that a *bean nighe* absorbs the energy of the dead in order to live and then transfer the leftovers back into the earth by the act of washing burial clothes in the stream."

"Don't let me forget where she is." Jane patted the bark. She knew when she stopped touching the tree her memory of her mother would fade. Such was part of the *bean nighe's* nature, a natural defense against discovery. It was why they were only known as myths. She turned to Iain. "How did you find me?"

"I knew ya needed me and I had to find ya. I heard your heart's call and took flight."

"And you transformed back. Twice. Your family made it sound as if that wasn't very likely to happen." She didn't even pretend to avert her eyes from the fact he was naked. "I like this look better than feathers." Jane crawled toward him. She wrapped her arms around his neck, knowing she didn't want to be anywhere else. Iain held her gently. "I'm glad you changed back. Earlier, I was close to locking you in a birdcage."

Iain gave a small laugh. "Ya just fought a *bean nighe* and ya want to discuss my shifting?"

"Iain," she whispered.

"What, love?" He stroked her cheek. As the *bean nighe* blood on his fingers touched her skin, the clarity came back.

"I just killed my mom." Power surged inside her, exhilarating and painful at the same time. "I did. I killed my *bean nighe* mom. She wanted me to take her place, which gives whole new meaning to joining the family business, but instead I transferred her into a tree." Jane gave a small, humorless laugh.

"Ya did what ya had to," Iain assured her.

"But, what if I become her now? What if she succeeded and I have to take her place."

A low moan sounded, interrupting them.

Jane stiffened. "Sean." How could she have forgotten her injured stepbrother?

They turned to the man lying on the ground. His head rolled back and forth. The run-in with the *bean nighe* had left Sean weakened. As he moved, the thick strands of his hair fell away, leaving him partially bald. Wrinkles fanned his eyes and lined his mouth.

"We should get him to a hospital," Jane said.

"If we must do anything, we can take him to Cait," Iain offered. "Keep this off the human radar."

"No. I don't want him anywhere near your family." Jane flinched as she tried to stand. "He is the reason the *bean nighe* had me in her grasp. He tried to trade me for his dead mother."

"Why would he want his dead mother?" Iain grimaced. "No good spells can come of that."

"I think he wanted her brought back to life."

Iain's frown deepened. "No good can come of reanimation of human remains. Zombies are not just something humans made up to scare each other."

"I don't think zombies were his intention either."

"No matter his plan, he meant ya harm. That I cannot forgive. Let him find his own way out of the forest. I'm taking ya home."

"Please, Iain. He's my stepbrother. We have to get him help."

Iain looked as if he'd refuse but then sighed and nodded. "For ya, love, I'll get him to the hospital, but only if ya promise to let me take ya to my home to let Cait tend your wounds."

"I'm fine."

"We don't know what your ma did to ya." Iain smoothed his hand over her hair before lifting a loose curl so she could see it. Her hair had turned white. "This is not negotiable."

Chapter Twenty-Two

"A *bean nighe's* daughter?" Cait eyed Jane's white hair. They were in the MacGregor library overlooking the outside gardens. Iain's aunt had just finished applying ointment to a large scrape on Jane's back.

Jane gingerly pulled the back of her shirt down, not liking the way it stuck to the ointment but refusing to walk around the mansion half naked.

"It would explain the air of death about ya," Margareta said. "And why ya see ghosts."

"Aye," Cait agreed. "And it explains your jagged lifeline if she was feeding off ya, and why those feedings didn't kill ya. Normally, they consume spirits. Ya said the doctors could never figure out why ya were sick."

"And the nature," Margareta added. "Plants grow from the fertilizer of other dead plants, and ya have the ability to renew and transfer life. Who knows what kind of powers ya will develop in time."

Jane shivered. She remembered what she'd told Iain about her mom, understood she needed to be physically touching her mom's energy to recall the details of her interactions with her, and she knew her mom's energy was now in a tree. What she didn't know is what it meant for her to be a half *bean nighe*. "Iain mentioned how a *bean nighe* is meant to consume ghosts and release their energy back into the world."

"Legend has it that *mnathan nighe*—that is, more than one *bean nighe*—are women who die with their baby in childbirth. Their spirits can't let go of the joy they expected to feel and their great disappointment. If such heightened emotion can turn the woman into a *bean nighe*, it would stand to reason the life of another child could somehow free her of it."

"How is that reasonable? A woman loses a child and her life, and so she is supposed sacrifice another child to end her curse?" Jane stood and began to pace.

"Oh, dear," Margareta chuckled. "Ya say that

like this is one of your American fairy tales. Have ya never read the old stories?"

"And not necessarily sacrifice. Ya are still here," Cait said. "Those poor *mnathan nighe* have a horrible fate—feeding off the dead, purging souls, cleaning what remains. Maybe ya were meant to take your ma's place. Maybe ya were meant to end her, as ya did. All I know is that ya must have been the key for your ma, and for her, death was a kindness."

"I was told my mother abandoned us," Jane argued. "My mother didn't die in childbirth. My father wouldn't have kept that from me."

"Oh, no," Margareta said. "A creature like her would have died centuries before ya were born. She would have to have been old to become so powerful. My guess is that she happened upon some mass tragedy and was able to gorge herself on it. From what I recall from my readings, a feast of souls would have shaken her out of her constant hunger and given her the power of consciousness long enough for her to seduce your father and give birth to ya. But I imagine the hunger would have been too hard to resist as it called her back to the graveyards. Consciousness couldn't be sustained forever before her nature to feed took over once more. Feeding off of ya probably gave her strength."

"So I'm becoming a *bean nighe*?" Jane touched her hair, evidence of her heritage. She tried to remember what the *bean nighe* had said to her, but aside from the knowledge that there had been a physical struggle, the words and thoughts were as faded as an old dream. Only vague impressions remained. "I'm going to turn into that thing and snack on ghosts?"

"Half *bean nighe*," Cait corrected. "We do not know what that means for ya."

Jane took a deep breath. As strange as this was, it was the best explanation she'd had for the events of her life so far. "So I'm not dying?"

"Euann, that little troll!" Malina declared from the doorway. "He got you too, Jane, did he?"

Jane turned, confused. "What do you mean?"

"Your hair. He put something in the shampoo." Malina gestured to the reoccurring white streak in her own hair. "Come with me. I'll show you how to cover it until it fades out completely, and then we'll hunt down—"

"Leave your brother alone, Malina," Margareta ordered. "He didn't do this."

"Who else? Euann did this to me," Malina pulled at her own locks.

"Jane was attacked by a *bean nighe*." Cait patted Jane's hair. "But she won."

"I miss all the fun." Malina pouted.

"The *bean nighe* was her ma," Margareta said with a bite of warning in her tone.

"Nothing a little hair color can't fix." Malina quickly changed the subject.

"I don't suppose you can work something a little more permanent? Like an anti-aging hair spell?" Jane had no desire to keep the white. "To take away my premature gray so I'm not coloring it for the rest of my life?"

"Come on, Jane. I'll get you fixed up," Malina said. "Though you kind of rock the whole banshee-chic. I have some magazines in my room. We can go shopping while your hair processes."

"YOU HAVE THE COOLEST POWER EVER." Jane's excited voice filtered out of Malina's bedroom.

Iain somehow knew he'd find her there. He'd felt her location the moment he'd entered his home.

"Oo, do this one," Jane said.

Curious, Iain pushed his finger against the door and let it silently open. He found Jane and his sister sitting in the middle of her room surrounded by an ocean of half-eaten cupcakes and pastries. An open recipe book lay on the floor between them. Both women were biting into cream puffs that matched the picture on the page. Their eyes turned toward him at the exact same moment, and they stopped mid-bite as if they'd been caught doing something incredibly bad.

Jane's hair was slicked into a pile on her head. A spot of brown hair color stained her forehead. She laughed as she bit down and chewed. She offered the rest of the cream puff to him. Iain stepped through the cupcake minefield, leaned over and took a bite without bothering to take it from her hand.

"Mm." He nodded before swallowing. "It's good."

"This is amazing," Jane said. "I show your sister a picture and she makes me food."

"Should I be jealous? Ya didn't get this excited by my powers," Iain said.

"You didn't tell me you could materialize cupcakes off a magazine picture," Jane said.

"That's because he can't," Malina informed. "Oh, and I didn't tell you the best part. You get all the pleasure of eating but none of the weight. On the down side, none of the nutrition if you're locked somewhere without actual food."

Jane dipped her finger in frosting and licked it. "Tastes real."

"She's like a battery," Malina said to Iain. She

set her cream puff down by a red velvet cupcake and began flipping through the magazine. She touched Jane, then a picture of a banket. Almost instantly, the pastry materialized between them. "Oh, oh, oh, I just had a brilliant idea. With my power and your battery charge, we should find a giant billboard. I think I saw one to the south of town with—"

"Stutzman Bakery," Jane finished for Malina. "The five-foot wedding cake!"

"All right, I'm cutting ya off," Iain said. "No five-foot wedding cakes."

"But…" Jane said, looking around the room. She pouted. "Giant billboard cake."

"Ya cannot eat a five-foot cake," Iain reasoned. "Not even if the rest of the MacGregor women helped ya."

"We could too," Malina said. "How hard could it be?" She counted on her fingers. "Me, Jane, ma, Cait, Lydia—"

Jane giggled. Her movements were a little jittery from the magickal sugar rush she had to be feeling. "This sounds like a challenge. I think we need to materialize the cake and prove Iain wrong."

"We have ourselves a wager." Malina jumped up. "I'll tell the others. Lads versus lasses."

Iain groaned.

Malina rushed out the door, only to come back and say to Jane, "You should wash that out now. Have Iain check the shampoo before ya use it to make sure Euann hasn't tampered with the bottle."

"Are you going to check my shampoo?" Jane grinned.

"Don't ya want to know about Sean?" Iain asked.

Jane smiled wider. "Yes. Tell me about Sean."

"Everything is handled. They admitted him for testing for the weakness. I explained that he was in town to see ya and that he hasn't gotten over his ma's death. Then, I induced Sean to put your name on the admittance form, giving ya access to his medical records so we can keep an eye on him. I'm not sure if it's a good thing, but if he tells them what happened, they'll think he suffered some kind of mental break."

"That's nice." Jane leaned over and dipped her finger into chocolate frosting and then licked it.

"Here, look at me." Iain lifted her chin and tipped back her head. Her eyes were glassy. "How much did ya eat?"

"I feel sparkly," she said.

"I see that." Iain chuckled and took advantage

of the closeness of her mouth. He kissed her, enjoying the taste of frosting on her lips.

"You feel sparkly too," she whispered.

"I think ya are drunk on magick," Iain said.

"Malina said the magick hair formula would cause me to be tingly." She gave a little frown. "Will you still like me if I have white hair forever?"

"Like ya?" Iain pulled her closer and kissed the tip of her nose. "Silly woman. Don't ya realize I love ya?"

"But I have to tell you…" Jane pulled away from him. "I'm half *bean nighe*, and I am scared I'm going to have to eat ghosts and do laundry."

"We should get this off your head now." Iain walked her down the hall toward his room. "I think the only thing ya have to worry about is eating a giant cake or risk losing a MacGregor bet."

"I like cupcakes," Jane said with a giggle. "Hey, I'm not going to die. I hope that doesn't change things between us."

"Glad to hear it, love." Iain made her walk faster. "I don't think I could survive it if ya died."

"I'm a battery."

"All right, love, all right." He pushed open his bedroom door and led her to his private bathroom.

"And you're my potato," she continued with a giggle.

Flicking his hand, he turned on the water without touching the knob. "Do ya think ya can handle a shower or do ya need assistance?"

Jane grabbed his face and kissed him. She didn't let go as she backed into the shower still wearing her clothes. She pressed her tongue between his lips. Her eager actions were inexact, clumsy even. His body hummed where she touched him. Warm water rushed over their clothing, sticking it erotically to their flesh.

"Melt the clothes," she ordered against his mouth.

As his magick stirred, he felt himself drawing power out of Jane to make it happen. He made their clothing slither off their body and pool into a wet pile at their feet. She gasped, throwing her head back in pleasure. Wet flesh slid against wet flesh as their bodies pressed together.

Iain turned her so that the stream of water hit her hair to rinse the concoction out of it. He pushed her hair back from her face. Jane tried to kiss his wrist as it passed close to her mouth. He chuckled at the action until he felt her hand wrapping his erection. A cloud formed over the shower and began to rain down on them, adding to the shower's water.

Iain glanced up in surprise. A tiny flash of lightning struck down toward them. Bagpipes sounded, a lively old song he hadn't heard in decades, perhaps longer. Jane pushed him back. Instead of the hard shower wall, his back hit the rough texture of a tree. The smell of wet grass and mud filled his nose. He didn't want her to stop.

Drums joined the bagpipes. The sound echoed from the distance. Iain grabbed Jane by the backs of her thighs and lifted her off the ground. She wrapped her legs around his waist, and he instantly kneeled. His knees hit the soft, wet bed of grass. He lowered her onto her back. Jane pulled his shoulders. Her legs slid along his naked hips. Iain entered her, joining his body to hers with one beautiful thrust.

They made love on the forest floor, surrounded by the sounds of his past, encouraged by the impossible storm raining down on them. Each plunge seemed to stir a strike of lightning and clap of thunder.

Suddenly, she stopped moving. Her eyes were clearer than before. She pushed his face away from her breast. "You said you love me."

"Aye. And ya said ya are a battery," he answered playfully.

"I love you too, Iain," she whispered. "I should have said it right away. I love you too."

Iain kissed her. "Aye, I know."

She laughed. The rain lightened. "You know?"

"Of course ya love me. I'm very loveable." He moved inside her, slower than before. Vines grew from the forest, stretching around them. He felt a tickle against his calf. Jane closed her eyes, moaning softly. He wanted to spend forever cocooned with her in their private world. Their pleasure built into the perfect climatic moment.

Almost instantly, the forest faded.

"Oh, ow," Jane arched beneath him. She lay on the hard tile of the shower floor. Iain pushed up to free her. She reached behind her and slid out the pile of wet clothes. Iain helped her to her feet. The shower stream continued to run hot as it hit them. "That was some trick. I really thought I was in the forest."

"That wasn't my doing," Iain said.

"Well, I know it wasn't me." Jane slid her arms around his neck and pulled him into a kiss.

As if to answer her, the tile on the shower wall cracked, and ivy curled in from the wall to reach toward her. It wound around her wrist and stopped. Jane lifted her arm. Iain gently pulled the vine off her and let it drop.

"It would seem I'm not the only one with

magick, nature girl." Iain shut off the water without touching the knob. "I'm glad to see you're feeling better though."

Jane touched her hair and then hurried naked and dripping with water to a mirror. She sighed in relief to see the dark color. "Yes. I'm feeling much better."

Chapter Twenty-Three

Jane stared at the side of the mansion. The English garden had gone wild, overtaking the exterior part of the house where Iain's bedroom was. "Not exactly the landscaping plan I had in mind."

Iain slid his hand onto her ass while looking at the overgrowth. "I'm changing my work order. I'd like do the whole house like this."

Jane laughed and pushed his hand off before anyone came out. "I bet you would."

"Ya must like having sex with me. That's some orgasm." Iain's smile widened. She could practically feel the male vanity oozing off of him.

Jane tapped him on the chest. "Easy there, laddie. That head of yours gets any bigger, and I won't be able to climb back into your bed."

"My head is plenty big." He glanced down at his waist meaningfully. "But I think ya can handle it, lassie."

"There ya are!" Euann appeared around the corner. "It's time."

"For?" Jane looked at Iain in confusion.

"Cake-eating challenge," Euann said. "Boys against girls. Ya called a MacGregor challenge, and it has been accepted. Terms have been set and agreed to. Now it's time to face the cake!"

"One cake billboard coming up." Rory appeared with Angus, Fergus, Murdoch, Raibeart and Malina. They carried the six-foot billboard sign for Stutzman Bakery and laid it on the ground.

"Shelly!" Raibeart yelled upon seeing her. "Where have ya been?"

"You stole a billboard?" Jane went to look down at it.

"What? Were we supposed to materialize cakes by the side of the road?" Malina smiled widely at Jane's expression. She breathed heavily from the exercise.

"For ya, my love," Raibeart declared with a pointed look at the billboard.

"Raibeart, that's Iain's Jane," Murdoch said, a hint of warning in his tone. "We discussed this."

"She'll always be my Shelly to me," Raibeart

answered, completely unconcerned. He winked at her.

"I don't think anyone ever told me what a *shellycoat* is," Jane said.

"Not important," Murdoch said. "You're not Shelly.

"A type of bogeyman who hangs around water," Malina answered. Then, giving a small laugh, she added, "I guess it's kind of like your *bean nighe* cousin."

Jane scrunched up her brow.

"I brought napkins," Cait announced. She stopped by the billboard and looked at the giant wedding cake. "That's larger than I imagined."

Jane touched Iain's arm. "They really don't expect to eat…"

"Hey, this is your idea." He shrugged. "A challenge is a challenge. Don't expect me to help ya. I'm on the boy team."

"But I was high on magick," Jane said.

"Never an excuse in the MacGregor clan," Euann countered.

"And MacGregors never back down from a challenge." Margareta appeared holding a tray filled with plates and forks. She paused, looking down at the sign. "Oh, Jane, we do need to discuss your wagers. As a MacGregor, ya have the right to a family challenge, but that is a lot of cake."

Jane stiffened. "I'm sorry, did you say I am a MacGregor?"

"Too soon? Did my son not propose yet?" Margareta gave Iain a stern look. "What are ya waiting for? Me to do it for ya? Marry this one. She saved your life. She'll put up with ya. We want to keep her."

"If Iain doesn't want her, I'll marry her for ya, Aunt Margareta," Rory offered.

"Kiss ass," Euann muttered.

"So, which tree exactly are we going to kill to make this challenge happen?" Fergus glanced around to a nearby box elder in contemplation.

"We don't need to kill anything," Malina said. "Jane is some kind of power conduit. She's like a battery that never runs out of juice."

"Wait, we can't do this now." Cait held up her hand.

Margareta also held up her hand. In unison with Cait, she turned toward the billboard on the ground. "A sign."

Jane frowned at the obvious statement.

"Euann, Malina, go drag Erik out of Lydia's embrace. Tell them I saw a sign. Invite Charlotte if Lydia will agree to have her veiled though I'm not sure Charlotte should have more magick done to her. We reconvene here in three hours. The rest of ya, follow me."

"Ya do it, banshee," Euann said to his sister. "Wait, I guess I can't call ya that now we have Jane. Ya do it, troll, I have to get the phone."

"Euann," Angus scolded. A few seconds later, a ringing sounded from inside. Euann ran ahead of the others as they went into the house to leave Iain and Jane outside.

"What is happening now?" Jane was confused. "I thought we were having an eating contest?"

"Reinforcements," Iain answered. "Or a refinement of terms. Who knows. It will keep them busy while I sneak ya back up to my room."

She leaned into him, liking the subtle hint of his cologne. "I'm starting to worry. What happens if we don't actually win the cake challenge?"

"Then ya pay the price, Shelly," Iain teased. "Either way, it looks like we have a couple of hours. I can help ya work up an appetite if ya want." He arched a brow and gave her a hopeful expression.

"Hey, Jane," Euann came out of the house holding his cell phone toward her. "It's for ya."

"On your phone?" Jane shook her head. "I don't—"

"House phone goes to Euann. He's the only one who will bother to answer it," Iain said. "I put this as your contact for the hospital."

Euann didn't cross the distance to her as he

said, "They want me to tell ya that Sean is stabilized and sleeping."

A pang of regret filled Jane at the news. She lifted her hand to indicate she heard him. Euann nodded and disappeared back into the house.

"Could you take me to the hospital? I know there's not much I can do, but I feel like I should check on Sean."

Iain instantly turned serious. "Let the doctors handle it. Ya have done all ya can for him. He tried to have ya killed, Jane."

"I can take myself. You don't have to go with me. I know what he did. I know what kind of a man he is." She didn't blame Iain for his anger. He cared about her. If the roles were reversed, she wouldn't want him going to see the person who'd tried to have him killed.

Iain took a deep breath. "I'll drive ya. But if he even looks at ya in a way I don't like…"

"I think maybe you should wait for me in the car." Jane threaded her arm into his. "If he tries anything, I'll go *bean nighe* on his ass and finish the job my mom started."

Chapter Twenty-Four

Sean glared at Jane from his hospital bed as the nurse left them alone. The thinning hairline and newly wrinkled skin aged him in such a way as to take what little power of charm he'd had. She'd witnessed it firsthand with the nurse. The boyish smile he flashed her showed yellow-stained teeth and ended up looking inappropriately creepy rather than charming and playful.

"Are you happy now?" he demanded. "You've taken everything from me. Have you come to kill me off and take my inheritance too?"

Jane stiffened at the unwarranted attack. Before she could stop herself, she quipped, "I came to give you a bill for the tomatoes you stole and gave to Mrs. Callister."

"I see. You've come to tarnish my good name

by calling me a thief." Sean snarled. He looked like he wanted to get out of the bed, but he didn't move.

"Would you prefer I call you an attempted murderer? Kidnapper?" Jane kept her voice soft. She didn't want the nurse to come back because the staff thought she was attacking their patient.

"Go away. Why are you even here?" Sean closed his eyes.

"I shouldn't have come." Jane tried to control her anger. She swallowed it into the pit of her stomach. "My ride is waiting outside. Get well soon, Sean." She walked toward the open door.

"Don't feel the need to come back, sis," he yelled after her. "You've done enough!"

Jane strode out of the room only to be stopped by the nurse. "Are you Sean's sister, Jane Turner, by chance?"

Jane frowned and thought about denying any connection. Finally, she sighed and nodded. "Yes, I'm his sister."

"He listed you as his contact person when he was admitted," the nurse said.

"Let me guess, he told you to give me the bill?"

The nurse reached over and pulled Sean's hospital room door closed. "You can't take his anger personally. We have set up a consultation with our Mental Health Services to help him through this transition. He's going to need family support."

"Transition?" Jane glanced toward the door. She hoped Sean had enough presence of mind to not rant about having his youth sucked away by a supernatural creature. "You mean because he's depressed? His mother recently passed and he hasn't been coping well. I'm sure that has something to do with his tiredness."

"I'm afraid it might be a little more serious than that. Depression definitely can be one cause of extreme fatigue, but taking into account the muscle degeneration, there are numerous potentially serious medical conditions we are concerned about. Have you talked with his doctor?"

Jane shook her head in denial and concentrated on the dark purple sleeve of the nurse's scrubs.

"We are keeping him for a workup since this may be a symptom of some medical concern." The nurse placed a hand on Jane's arm. "But I don't want you to worry. He's under the best care. The doctor has ordered a comprehensive workup."

Jane didn't know how to respond. She really couldn't say Sean had been attacked by a *bean nighe.*

"Jane?" Iain appeared behind her, startling her. "What happened? I know ya asked me to stay in the car, but I was worried about ya."

The nurse looked expectantly at Iain as he joined them.

"It's ok. This is my, ah…"

"I'm her fiancé," Iain stated as if it was the most natural assertion in the world. Jane inhaled sharply and looked up at him. Iain smiled and put his arm around her.

"So Sean's muscles are bad?" Jane asked, glad to have Iain's comfort. "You don't think he'll recover?"

"His symptoms could be caused by Guillain-Barré syndrome, multiple sclerosis or a subdural hematoma due to a head injury. He indicated he fell." The nurse tilted her head, pausing as she forced Jane to look at her. "He is going to need a wheelchair, at the very least in the short term. He's also going to need care. We have people you can talk to as you make preparations."

"Care?" Jane shook her head in denial. If this was some kind of cosmic test, she was about to fail. Jane held up her hand. "I don't think—"

"We'll see to it he has the best care," Iain interrupted. He lifted his hand and made a small gesture. "Thank ya, nurse."

The nurse smiled and instantly left.

"I guess he can stay with me," Jane said, hating the words, but what else could she do? Before Iain could say anything, she went back into Sean's room. She felt Iain follow her.

"What do you want?" Sean demanded as Jane entered. "I thought I told you to leave."

"Sean, stop. I'm not here to fight with you." Jane glanced back at Iain. He crossed his arms over his chest but nodded at her in support. To her brother, she continued, "I shouldn't have yelled earlier. I came to check on you to make sure you're all right."

"Let's see. A banshee ate my mother's spirit after most likely killing her, then tried to kill me, and all because you ran away from your responsibilities." Sean hit his hand down on his thigh. "And now I'm in this bed and you're here, looking healthier than ever. How is that fair? You're supposed to be the sick one. I was doing you a favor coming here and helping you."

"Help me? By guilting me? Scaring me? Sacrificing me?" Jane shook her head in disbelief.

"Just go." Sean turned his head in dismissal. "Take your manwhore with you."

"Say what ya like about me, but speak to your sister with respect. I don't see anyone else coming to visit ya," Iain pointed out.

"The nurse said you're going to need home

health care, at the very least in the short term. For better or worse, you are family. You can come stay with me while you heal," Jane offered. Sean might not deserve her consideration, but she had to try. "We'll figure something out. Whatever happens, you don't have to go through it alone."

"I know what you want. You want the money mother left me. You're mad that your father loved her more than you and left her everything." Sean became rigid. "I would rather burn in the fiery pits of hell than stay another minute in your presence. It should be you in this bed."

Jane saw the anger and hatred in him. She witnessed the undeserving entitlement. His words stung, but they also freed her. She couldn't help someone who didn't want her help. Sean had come into her life and disrupted it, not the other way around. She hadn't invited him. She hadn't asked for it. Taking a deep breath, she said, "Goodbye, Sean. I hope you heal."

Iain guided his arm behind her back as she left the room as if to protect her from the angry vibes shooting off Sean's very being.

As they made it down the hall, she said, "I'm surprised you didn't try to stop me from offering."

"Ya don't seem to appreciate it when I try to tell ya what to do. I may have some overprotective qualities, but I'm trainable." He gave her a small smile.

His light teasing worked. Jane returned the look and wrapped her arm around his waist as they walked.

Iain hooked his arm around her shoulders. "My family donates to several facilities. We'll make sure Sean gets treatment as long as ya wish."

"Thank you—oh, man, that woman is like a bad penny that keeps turning up." Jane tried to change direction as she saw Mrs. Callister at the front desk. Iain didn't let her. "What does she do? Make the rounds to see who has what illness?"

"One second." Iain let her go and strode to the woman. Mrs. Callister blinked in surprise at his sudden approach. With a devil-may-care smile and a slightly thickened accent, he inquired, "Ya still have that book ya carry around?"

Mrs. Callister appeared confused but slowly nodded.

"Write this down," Iain instructed. Mrs. Callister pulled the notepad and pencil out of her purse. "Jane is going to marry me. I'm going to try to convince her to have twelve children and a dog. And her tomatoes cost three dollars and fifty cents a pound."

Mrs. Callister's pencil didn't move.

"Have a nice day." Iain tilted his head before

offering his arm to Jane to walk her out of the hospital.

"Did you just include Mrs. Callister in your marriage proposal to me?" Jane asked as they walked the long sidewalk through the manicured lawn to the parking lot.

"Technically, the nurse. Ya didn't protest when I called myself your fiancé so that counts as an agreement and I'm holding ya to it. And if ya want quibble over details, my ma is already doing the wedding plans, and ya didn't protest that." Iain grabbed her hand and stopped walking, pulling her out of her forward momentum and into his chest.

"I thought that was Erik's wedding," Jane said.

"Ya are everything to me, Jane. Even if ya don't ever walk down that aisle to be my wife, I belong to ya. It's that simple, and I don't care who knows it."

Jane kissed him. Love and happiness filled her. And then there was hope. Hope in a future. Hope in a life without sickness. Hope in a fate greater and bigger than she'd ever imagined.

Iain held her tightly in the safety of his embrace. Without looking to see what was happening, she felt his magick surging through her, radiating from them to bloom flowers and lengthen the grass. Finally, when she pulled away, she looked up into his loving eyes. She could spend an eternity with him, and it wouldn't be enough.

"Let's go home." He tried to continue walking down the sidewalk, but she held him tighter.

"Iain," she whispered. "I have to tell you something important."

"What is it, love?" His expression fell in concern.

"My tomatoes are only two dollars a pound."

Chapter Twenty-Five

Jane stared at the expansive lawn covered with giant food billboards—a plate of two-foot buffalo wings, three-quarters of a five-foot pizza, a three-foot beer bottle, gigantic cheese curds and a… boxer puppy ten times the normal size?

"Ah…" Jane pointed at the dog in confusion. Iain gestured his hands to the side, indicating he didn't know.

"I want to name him Jim," Rory announced. "He's so cute."

Jane sighed in relief. "Oh, thank goodness. For a second, I thought you wanted to, um, never mind."

"Da wants to see you upstairs, Iain." Malina strode from the house. The mansion door had been left open. While they were at the hospital, the MacGregors had been busy setting up outdoor dining tables and stealing billboards.

"Don't start eating without me." Iain kissed Jane's cheek.

"I can't make you a giant puppy," Malina told Rory. "Even if I could, he'd grow up to be an even bigger dog. You can barely take care of yourself."

"But Niall gets his pet lizard," Rory protested.

"No." Malina shook her head. She hooked her arm into Jane's. "Come with me."

"But we still get to have the giant feast, right?" Rory yelled after the women.

"Sorry about them." Malina led Jane into the house and through the dining room. "They became a little too excited when they found out we can make giant food without killing the entire forest."

"Too bad it has no nutritional value," Jane said. "Together, we could feed the world."

"We're already working on it." Malina let go of Jane's arm and continued up the stairs. "Uncle Raibeart founded a MacGregor charity, whose purpose to feed underprivileged families all over the world. We keep a low profile and off the various government radars. Raibeart feels politicians just get in the way of good deeds. Then again, he remembers the feudal system from personal experience."

"Raibeart founded a charity?" Jane tried to stop her surprise from showing.

"I know, right? He hardly seems capable of dressing himself in the morning."

"So what's up? Where are we going?" Jane took the stairs slowly.

"We have a surprise for you." Malina grinned. When they reached the stairs, she grabbed Jane's hand and practically ran down the hall, pulling Jane behind her into one of the bedrooms. They came to a full-length antique mirror. "Follow me." Malina stepped through the glass front and disappeared. However, she didn't let go of Jane's hand, and Jane was pulled through after her.

Jane closed her eyes tightly and held her breath as she passed through the warm glass. They surfaced on the other side in a small bedroom that did not belong in the MacGregor mansion. Lydia Barratt examined her reflection. She wore an elegant lace wedding dress. Cait and Margareta waited behind her with wide smiles and clutched hands.

"You look beautiful," Jane said.

"So will you." Lydia picked up a bridal magazine and handed it to Jane. "Choose quickly, before Charlotte wanders back into the house. She can't know about the magick."

"Choose?" Jane asked in confusion.

"Pick your dress," Cait said.

"My dress?" Jane slowly took the magazine.

"Double wedding," Lydia said in excitement. "The elders saw a sign."

"Surprise! Welcome to the twelfth century. You're getting married today, and no one asked you if that's what you wanted." Malina smirked, clearly finding amusement in the circumstances.

"The sign was clear," Margareta said. "Today is a good day for weddings. We cannot ignore the signs. Ya never know when ya will see another."

"The sign was a giant billboard my family committed a felony to get," Malina said, not losing her mischievous smile.

Margareta sighed and looked annoyed. "Ya never listen to the signs, Malina, but even this one should be obvious to ya. A wedding billboard for a MacGregor challenge made by the unknowing bride. We all know that MacGregor men can be a challenge. It must be done today if there is to be happiness in these marriages."

"Now?" Jane's hand shook as she held the magazine.

"I know it's a lot to take in," Margareta said, "but the magick is clear. It doesn't take future casting to see how much my boys love ya two."

"I wish Charlotte could come. She's my best

friend." Lydia frowned at her reflection. "She should be my maid-of-honor."

"Charlotte is delicate right now and, though we can veil her from seeing the magick, I'm not sure that's the best idea," Margareta said. "Her mental health must come first."

"Tell her your new mother-in-law was overbearing with the wedding plans and you decided to elope," Malina suggested. "She'll believe that."

Jane took a deep breath. The full impact of possibilities hit her. She could have a full life, a family, children, a husband. Iain.

"Jane?" Malina asked, concerned. "What's wrong?"

"I'm going to live." Jane moved her gaze over the other women. "Really live."

"Aye, dear, for a very long time," Cait said. "Practically an eternity."

"Iain will give ya his power," Margareta explained. "His love will recharge ya, extending your years and—"

"It's not as romantic as all that," Malina interrupted. "It's a way to make you non-natural-born-magicks keep up with us. After a while, you won't need to be around him all the time. You'll build up reserves to help your own lifespan and magickal gifts. Until that happens, you'll need to be around your husbands almost constantly."

Malina arched a brow. "Are you sure you two want to marry my brothers? I mean, they—"

"Malina!" Margareta scolded. She flung her hand at her daughter. Jane gasped as she felt the woman drawing energy out of her to make the magick happen. Malina's body flung back, flying through the mirror and disappearing. Margareta retracted her fingers and laughed. "Ya are a battery, Jane. Perhaps ya will not need Iain's magick. There seems to be perks to being half *bean nighe.*"

"Where did she go?" Lydia asked.

Margareta went to the portal mirror and stuck her head in. "She's fine. A little dazed. I simply willed her out of here so she could rethink her attitude." She clapped her hands and smiled. "Now, where were we? Oh, aye." She reached for the magazine Lydia held. "Time to pick your dress."

Chapter Twenty-Six

Iain was sure he'd never felt as amazing as he did in this moment, or as scared. When he went up to see his father, it was to find the MacGregor elders waiting with Erik. His brother wore his finest kilt and formal jacket.

"Put this on," Angus told Iain, thrusting a formal tux at him. "Ya can't wear jeans to your own wedding."

"Always do what your wife says," Fergus advised the grooms.

"Always *pretend* to do what she says," Angus corrected. "But don't get caught disobeying. Your ma keeps a tally in her head of things I've done. After a few hundred years, those tallies add up."

"I disappear for a few days and everything has changed with ya." Erik brushed his hand down

Iain's chest, dusting off his jacket. "Can ya believe we're to have a double wedding?" Erik paused. "Did ya remember to propose to her? Apparently, the women like it when ya propose."

"More or less." Iain smiled to himself. He loved how uncomplicated Jane was. She didn't demand anything from him and yet gave him so much by her very nearness. He'd seen the big heart in her when she'd offered to take her step-brother into her home. Not many people would forgive so quickly. Iain wasn't sure he could ever be so forgiving.

Erik frowned. "That wasn't a joke, Iain. Lydia almost left me because I did not respect her by asking her to marry me before assuming she would. Do not start your marriage wrong."

Iain saw Erik's unusually serious expression. His smile fell. Without stopping to think about what he was doing, he ran from the room.

"Iain, your kilt," Angus yelled.

Iain let his feelings guide him as he sought out Jane. He found her in the backyard standing next to a buffet of giant food. Members of his family were there, but he ignored them all. The sight of Jane in a white mermaid dress took his breath away. The skirt hugged her hips and thighs, only to flare at the bottom. Her curly hair piled on her head, revealing the nape of her neck and the slope of her shoulders.

"Iain?" someone said his name, but he didn't pay attention.

Jane turned at the sound to look at him. "Iain? What's wrong? What's—"

Iain strode to her. He cupped her face and looked into her eyes. "I respect ya."

"Uh, thank you. I respect you too," she said.

"From the moment I first saw ya, my world stopped. Time meant nothing." His love for her poured out of him. "I may not do things the right way, but know I respect ya and…"

"You trust me," Jane said. "I know. You told me."

"And I love ya. I want to marry ya. Marry me, Jane." Iain let go of her face and quickly kneeled.

"I thought that was what we were doing." Jane pulled at his arm to get him to stand. "This dress isn't really my everyday gardening attire."

"I'm proposing. Ya have to say ya will marry me. I don't want to start our marriage wrong."

"Yes, Iain, I will marry you in a few minutes in this dress with your family as witnesses." Jane gave a small laugh, stopping him from kissing her. "On two conditions."

"Anything, love, anything."

"You unfreeze your family." Jane glanced to the side.

Iain had managed to stop time again, just like the day he'd found her at her nursery. He hadn't meant to. He wanted to be alone with his bride and so his magick had made it happen. His ma stood nearby, her mouth open in mid-sentence. Rory was gesturing to the billboard of the giant puppy while entreating a cross-armed Malina. Euann was grinning at a bridal Lydia while Angus stood poised to smack him on the back of the head for most likely flirting with his brother's fiancée. "And the other condition?"

Jane laughed harder. "You put on some pants for the ceremony."

Iain glanced down in surprise to realize he'd left his kilt upstairs. He stood in his boxer-briefs. "I wasn't done changing. What? Ya don't like my legs?" He turned and thrust his ass to the side to give her full view of his goods.

Jane tilted her head to the side and smiled. She gave his ass a little smack. "Lime-green boxers are an interesting choice with this tux jacket. But this wasn't what I picture you wearing under your kilt."

"It's not." He winked. "I told ya, I wasn't finished getting ready." He pulled at his waist band and started to inch them down his hips. "I can show ya if ya like."

Jane put her hands over his and stopped him from disrobing on the back lawn. She glanced to his frozen family and laughed. "Lime green boxers it is. I guess I can try to explain the wedding pictures to our children later."

"Ah, *fíorghrá*, our children will be MacGregors. Trust me, ya will have a lot more to explain away than this." Suddenly, he stiffened and looked down at her stomach. A slow smile found its way to his stunned expression. Excitement filled him. "Wait, are ya trying to tell me that ya are…?"

"What?" Jane followed his eyes down. "Pregnant? No. No, I'm not. I—"

Iain silenced her with a deep kiss. When she was relaxed fully against him, he said, "Not to worry, love, if ya want babies, we can start working on that just as soon as ya are done losing the post-wedding eating contest. And I promise ya—" he cupped her ass, pulled her toward his erection and lightly circled his hips so she'd get his obvious meaning, "—I will work tirelessly to make sure that happens." Humming lightly, he held her tighter. The pressure of her felt wonderful against him. "I wish we could start now. I'm torn between my two desires—the desire to make ya my wife for eternity and the desire to cart ya upstairs and…" He paused, running a finger along the top of her bodice while keeping one hand firmly in place on her backside. He let the digit bounce lightly on her soft cleavage a few inches above where her nipple was hidden. "Rip ya out of this dress, throw ya on our bed and get started on our two-month horizontal honeymoon."

Jane's breathing visibly deepened.

Using his most persuasive voice, he whispered against her neck, "How about we sneak away for a practice round?"

"Mm, too bad you can't also fast-forward time," Jane teased. "That way we could do both, get married and—"

JANE GASPED as the world blurred. She felt herself ripped out of Iain's embrace and flung forward into a rapid motion she couldn't control. The actions were almost too much for her to mentally process as they happened. Jane sped up a grass aisle with Lydia, meeting their future husbands at the end. Iain kissed her, the moment brief and interrupted by the protests of his family to get on with the ceremony.

Raibeart spoke words in a slur of Gaelic from an old leather-bound text. Purple and white light shot up from the book to rain down upon them. Next she was being swung in circles as Iain danced her around the lawn. There was laughter and joking, and someone set a tablecloth on fire. The taste of cake filled her mouth before being replaced by the insistent pressure of Iain's hot kisses.

It seemed like only seconds had passed, squished full of hours. Kissing turned to something more, and Jane cried out as she came out of fast-forward. They were in Iain's room, her new husband's body on top of her. The first thrust filled her as reality completely returned.

Jane grabbed his arm. The soft mattress molded along her back. "What just happened?"

Iain looked as stunned as she. Then he smiled. "Hello, my wife."

"Did you just fast-forward through our wedding so we could…" Jane's attention moved from her disorientation to her stomach. Iain rocked, causing her to lose her focus. "So…we…"

He held her thigh against his waist and flexed his hips. Her body accepted him, already heated to near climax.

"My wife," Iain whispered over and over as if amazed by the fact. "My wife. My wife. My beautiful wife."

Energy hummed inside her, pure magick. She

felt the life outside of the bedroom stirring and growing, delicate as a blooming flower and yet as strong as a tree. Iain's love radiated through her. Her hands trembled as she caressed his body. Snaps of electricity joined the tips of her fingers to his chest and arms, and twinkling lights danced over the bed. The feelings overwhelmed as pleasure built. All thoughts left her as they found their climax in unison.

In the aftermath, as she lay in his arms, she said, "I can't believe you made me miss my wedding."

"Ya were there love. It happened. The memories will fill in." He kissed her temple. "And for the record, it was ya who willed us to fast-forward time so we could make love—not that I'm complaining."

"Nice try, warlock," Jane countered. Just as she was about to tease him, her stomach made a strange noise. She groaned. It felt as if she'd swallowed a bowling ball. "Oh, damn, I'm remembering the cake-eating contest. Why didn't you stop me?"

"And be accused of tampering with the results? Not a chance."

"At least the girls won." Jane drew her legs up to her chest.

"Think again," Iain countered. He placed his

hand on her stomach. Warmth filled her, instantly calming her churning insides. When she again relaxed, he said, "Ya lost."

Jane reached to touch his face. "No, I believe I actually won. You are mine. I love you, Iain." She gave a small laugh. "And from what I understand, you can never escape me. You are stuck with me forever."

"Why would I want to escape?" Iain pulled her close. "Though, I think once the men collect on our challenge win, I will be the clear winner here."

Jane paused halfway to kissing him and pulled back. "Wait. What were those terms again, exactly? I don't think anyone ever said."

Iain laughed. "Don't worry. Ya will find out your punishment soon enough."

Jane's response was lost in his kiss as he began to make love to her slowly. Soon, the world again faded and nothing mattered but the fact she was in Iain's arms. Forever.

Chapter Twenty-Seven

EPILOGUE

"Are we really going to do this?" Lydia hugged her arms and eyed the other MacGregor women.

"A bet is a bet," Cait said, not looking too happy as she unbuttoned her sweater. "If we don't, we'll never hear the end of it. They seem to think this will excuse their constant midnight mischief."

"Or explain it enough so that we no longer protest their fun," Margareta added.

"But are they going to watch?" Jane glanced to the men standing on the front lawn. She refused to take off her clothing in front of Iain's male relatives.

"Oh, don't ya worry about that, love," Margareta said. "I baked a little something special into the cookies and left them on the table with a note that said not to touch them. I guarantee every man over there stole at least one."

"Hey, everything is blurry." Malina weaved on her feet and began waving her hand slowly in front of her face and giggling. "I taste like purple sunshine."

"And apparently my daughter did as well." Margareta gave Malina a disapproving look. Malina didn't notice.

Jane glanced behind her to the men on the lawn. They were in various states of distraction. Rory sat on the grass, petting the shards and calling them Jim. Murdoch and Euann chased imaginary butterflies. Niall stood with his arms crossed, looking very sternly…at a tree. Erik and Iain pretended to sword fight.

"Did you drug them?" Jane asked.

Margareta chuckled. "A little magick in the cookie dough. It's perfectly harmless. And the best part is Euann won't be sending out a mass video text message to the family of our activities."

Cait took Jane's hand and lifted her palm toward the men. She borrowed energy from Jane to make vines grow up from the ground to create shackles around their legs. The men didn't notice. "They'll be tethered to their areas until we get back. No wandering off."

"Ladies, shall we run?" Margareta asked.

Cait, smiling a little more now, shrugged out of her pin skirt. "Into the night with us."

"I'm a unicorn rainbow," Malina yelled, running in circles. "Follow me into the forest! I know the way!" She didn't change course as she continued to loop.

Jane shook her head, even as she pulled off her shirt. What did she get herself into falling in love with this family? She glanced back at the sword-fighting Iain and smiled. Perfection. That's what she had. Pure and utter perfection.

Grabbing Malina's hand, Jane said, "Come on, unicorn rainbow. You heard the lady. Into the night with us!"

The End

The Series Continues...

WARLOCKS MACGREGOR® 3: STIRRING UP TROUBLE

Magick, Mischief and Kilts.
Some Warlocks excel at brewing up trouble.

Warning: Contains yummy, hot, mischievous MacGregor boys who may or may not be wearing clothing and who are almost certainly up to no good on their quest to find true love.

For more information, visit
www.MichellePillow.com

Warlocks MacGregor® 3: Stirring Up Trouble Extended Excerpt

Winter, 1591, England-Scotland Border
"Do not leave me." The pain was unbearable

in that moment of waiting, of knowing the end was near, knowing these were the last seconds he would have with his Elspeth. Tears streamed down his love's face as he reached for her in the snow. This was not how their life together was supposed to go. They were supposed to be immortal. They were supposed to have each other forever.

All of Fergus MacGregor's warlock powers could not make time last. That didn't mean he didn't try. He cast every spell he knew, and even some he didn't. He willed time to stop, and for a short while, it stalled.

The trickle of blood streaming along her pale cheek slowed until it barely traveled over her flesh. Her eyes shone with pain. To keep her in this state was too cruel. She was locked in agony. There was no spell he knew of that could transfer her death into him. Yet he tried to do that too.

"I'm coming with ya, my heart," Fergus said, more like a plea. He let his powers slip from her, unable to prolong her suffering any longer. He felt around for his sword only to discover he'd dropped it several feet away. He reached his hand out, using his magick to call it to him. The blade began to slide in the snow only to stop when his wife's voice interrupted his action.

"Malina," Elspeth whispered, making him

think of their niece. The baby was silent, her cry bound with a spell. "Protect."

How could he deny the desperate need in her gaze? Fergus nodded. "Aye."

"Whatever is beyond, find me again," she whispered. Her bloodstained lips opened a few times as if she would say more, but the life ebbed from her.

"Elspeth?" Fergus stared at her chest, waiting for it to rise. Just one more breath. One more word. One more kiss. One more moment. One more...

She didn't move.

Pain racked over him, crippling him with death's cruelty. This was not how it was meant to be. Seven years. That's all they'd had. They were supposed to have eternity.

"*Gráim thú*. I promise, Elspeth," Fergus whispered, gathering her into his arms. "Whatever lies ahead, I'll find ya."

Warlocks MacGregor® Series

Love Potions
Spellbound
Stirring Up Trouble
Cauldrons and Confessions

The Series Continues...

Spirits and Spells
Kisses and Curses
Magick and Mischief
A Dash of Destiny

More Coming Soon

Visit www.MichellePillow.com for details.

About Michelle M. Pillow

New York Times & *USA TODAY* Bestselling Author

Michelle loves to travel and try new things, whether it's a paranormal investigation of an old Vaudeville Theatre or climbing Mayan temples in Belize. She believes life is an adventure fueled by copious amounts of coffee.

Newly relocated to the American South, Michelle is involved in various film and documentary projects with her talented director husband. She is mom to a fantastic artist. And she's managed by a dog and cat who make sure she's meeting her deadlines.

For the most part she can be found wearing pajama pants and working in her office. There may or may not be dancing. It's all part of the creative process.

~

**Come say hello! Michelle loves talking
with readers on social media!**

www.MichellePillow.com

facebook.com/AuthorMichellePillow

twitter.com/michellepillow

instagram.com/michellempillow

bookbub.com/authors/michelle-m-pillow

goodreads.com/Michelle_Pillow

amazon.com/author/michellepillow

youtube.com/michellepillow

pinterest.com/michellepillow

Newsletter

To stay informed about when a new book in the series installments is released, sign up for updates:

Sign up for Michelle's Newsletter
michellepillow.com/author-updates

Complimentary Material

The Dragon's Queen

BY MICHELLE M. PILLOW

Dragon Lords Series
Bestselling Shapeshifter Romance

Mede of the Draig knows three things for a fact: As the only female dragon shifter of her people, she is special. She can kick the backside of any man. And she absolutely doesn't want to marry.

Mede has spent a lifetime trying to prove herself as strong as any male warrior. Unfortunately, being the special, rare creature she is, she's been claimed as the future bride to nearly three dozen Draig—each one confident that when they come for her hand in marriage fate will choose them. When the men aren't bragging about how they're going to marry her, they're acting like she's a delicate rare flower in need of their protection.

She is far from a shrinking solarflower.

Prince Llyr of the Draig knows four things for a fact: He is the future king of the dragon shifters. He must act honorably in all ways. He absolutely, positively is meant to marry Lady Mede. And she dead set against marriage.

Llyr's fate rests in the hands of a woman determined not to have any man. With a new threat emerging amongst their cat shifting neighbors, a threat whose eyes are focused firmly on Mede, time may be running out. It is up to him to convince her to be his dragon queen.

The Dragon's Queen Excerpt

There were three things Medellyn knew for a fact. She was special. She could kick the ass of any boy. And she did not want to marry and have babies.

She was special.

Medellyn was one of the only dragon shifting females in all the universe, and definitely in all of the Draig. Only once in a thousand births was a female dragon shifter born. She was rare, or so everyone kept telling her. Her childhood was a strange contradiction. Her very proper mother tried to treat her as if she were some sacred crystal that might crack. Her warrior father tried to make her train like a boy while dressing like a girl.

She could kick the ass of any boy.

Medellyn hated when boys tried to act as if she were weak and to be protected. Her dragon was just as fierce as any of theirs, probably more so. To prove her point, she'd gladly pummel any who had challenged her to the ground...and some who hadn't.

She *absolutely, positively* did not want to marry and have babies.

Being the special, rare creature she was, in the twenty not-so-sweet girlhood years of her life she'd been claimed as the future bride to nearly three dozen boys—each one confident that when they came of the age to marry she would make their crystals glow and they hers.

Glowing crystals wasn't just a metaphor. On the day she was born, her father journeyed to Crystal Lake like all the new fathers did. He dove beneath the waves, swam down to the deepest part and pulled her stone from the lakebed. Like all Draig children, she wore the stone around her neck, and would continue to wear it until the day it glowed telling her which of the dragon shifting men she was destined by the gods to marry. Okay, technically she might be destined to marry an offworlder like most Draig men, but no one on her planet seemed to think so.

Gods bones, she hoped she wasn't destined to end up with any of the idiots on her planet. They had yet to impress her.

When it was her turn to go to the Breeding Festival, the crystal would glow signifying her *curse* for all to see. Well, her "blessing" as her mother called it. Lady Grace did not appreciate her daughter calling marriage a curse. Grace did not appreciate a lot of things that Medellyn liked, such as swords and bows, ceffyl riding, camping alone in the forest, hunting, sparring, smashing arrogant looks off of dragon men's faces.

It was a fight with her mother that sent her running through the mountain forest. Medellyn hated the woman, hated what her mother wanted her daughter to be. Grace was only a human, brought to their planet as a bartered bride. She married Medellyn's father without question and spent most of her days completely in docile agree-ment with whatever her husband said. Medellyn couldn't imagine taking anyone else's opinions over her own.

Her father, Axell, was a highly praised warrior in the Draig army and carried the title of Top Breeder of the ceffyls. The man's whole life focused on four things: his wife, his only child, and mares and steeds. Her father was a very important man, but his work kept him away from home several nights a week as he slept outdoors with the herd. With a three-year gestation period and only about fifty percent live-birth rate, the animals were not a resource that could be easily renewed. His ceffyls supplied the soldiers with mounts and farmers used them for beasts of burden to help with the fields.

Like Axell, Medellyn was a proud dragon. Had she been born male, she would have been a warrior, too. Instead, she was *special*. How could her human mother begin to understand the wildness than ran in her dragon blood? If she had, Grace would never have asked Medellyn to tame her spirit.

Breathing hard, she came to an abrupt halt and screamed into the trees. Her body shook with rage and she tore at the pretty gown she wore. She hated her body, hated being special, hated being expected to act like a lady when she felt like a dragon. Her taloned finger snagged on the crystal around her neck and she cut the leather strap of the necklace. The crystal flew several fect away.

"I am not some man's chattel," she yelled, knowing she'd run far enough away that her mother could not hear her retorts. Since she was shifted her voice was hoarse and powerful, and she reveled in the fierceness of it. "I am not some breeding ceffyl to have children. It is not my place to give you fifty grandkids. I can't help you only had one child. If you would have made me a boy, I wouldn't be a disappointment to you!"

Tears stung her eyes as Medellyn walked aimlessly, searching the forest floor for the fallen necklace. Finding it, she grabbed the inert crystal into her fist. It was a reminder of all she was expected to be. She took a deep breath, looking at her fist and then to the stones littering the forest floor. A small smile formed on her mouth. Medellyn dropped the crystal on the hard ground and glared at it. Rage boiled inside her, the kind of rage surely only a dragon shifter could feel.

"This is what I think of your fate," she growled as she fell to her knees.

Medellyn grabbed a heavy rock and smashed it down onto her necklace. The crystal cracked. The noise gave her some satisfaction so she hit it again. Grunting with each strike of the stone, she didn't stop until her future had been ground to dust.

"That is what I think of your destiny."

To find out more about Michelle's books
visit www.MichellePillow.com

Please Leave a Review

THANK YOU FOR READING!

Please take a moment to share your thoughts by
reviewing this book.

Be sure to check out Michelle's other titles at
www.MichellePillow.com

CPSIA information can be obtained
at www.ICGtesting.com
Printed in the USA
LVHW030816191220
674602LV00039B/527

9 781625 011657